A

CANDLELIGHT REGENCY SPECIAL

Candlelight Regencies

REBEL IN LOVE

Veronica Howard

A CANDLELIGHT REGENCY SPECIAL

Published by
Dell Publishing Co., Inc.
1 Dag Hammarskjold Plaza
New York, New York 10017

Dell ® TM 681510, Dell Publishing Co., Inc.

ISBN: 0-440-17423-6

Printed in the United States of America

First printing—May 1981

CHAPTER ONE

"My dear Lucius, you always were excessively absent-minded, but I do declare that over the years you have become positively fuddle-headed!"

Lady Hensham surveyed her cousin across the dilapidated library, her darting eyes noting its threadbare carpet, its shelf-lined walls of dusty tomes, and the general air of neglect and decay.

Lucius Glaybourne blinked uncertainly at her, removed his spectacles, and sighed heavily.

"You are probably quite right, my dear. I barely notice anymore how the time flies."

"You're too immersed in ancient history, Lucius." Lady Hensham viewed with distaste the mountain of reference books on his desk. "I could understand your disinclination to surface into this modern world of ours if you had only yourself to bother about, but—that dear child Halcyon; how is she faring?"

Lucius had the grace to look ashamed.

"Time passes so quickly," he reiterated, as though seeking to mitigate his cousin's censure. "Why," he laughed hesitantly, "it gave me quite a turn to see you sail into the library just now. I had thought you to be still in Europe, don't you know."

Lady Hensham magnanimously ignored his rather dubious reference to her stately deportment.

"Pshaw! It's seven years since we went to Europe —and I have warned you consistently in my letters

5

to be ready for my return. Letters, I might add, that were never acknowledged or answered," she added with some asperity. "Besides, as you would have known if you'd read my letters, I've been back in England for a month, long enough to reestablish my household in Bath."

"Yes . . . well . . . er—"

"Lucius, really! You are quite beyond redemption! She looked around her. "But where is Halcyon? I had thought to come across her in the house as I—*sailed*—through looking for you."

She had thought to meet someone at least in the halls. But not only had there been no answer to her urgent knocking on the rotting oak door, which barely clung to its hinges, neither had she encountered any servants in the dusty, rambling old house.

Lucius waved vaguely in the direction of the garden. "Halcyon? She'll be out there somewhere, I imagine. But why would you want her, my dear?" ·

Lady Hensham whirled around in dismay.

"Can you really have forgotten, Lucius? Were not my letters sufficient reminder to you that this is Halcyon's seventeenth year, and the time has come for her promised betrothal to—"

"Egad! I had quite forgot!"

"But did not Halcyon remind you?"

"I . . ." Lucius fumbled with the papers in his desk. "My dear—" He broke off again, leaving his cousin in no doubt as to the root of his discomfiture.

"You don't—you *can't* mean that she doesn't know? Am I to understand that you never told her?"

"Didn't bother to inform her at first when the agreement was made . . . She was too young, you understand."

"And later?"

"Damned if the matter didn't quite slip my memory," he mumbled.

"Oooh!" wailed Lady Hensham as uncharacteristic hysteria mounted in her breast. "What a shuttle-brain you are! The girl will scarcely take kindly to having the news sprung upon her quite so suddenly. Still," she consoled herself, "as a dutiful daughter, and one who is, I am sure, obedient to her father's wishes, she will no doubt—" Something in her cousin's face communicated his skepticism to her. "Lucius! Why are you looking at me like that? Regrettable and deplorable though your omission may be, surely it is something that can be speedily and easily rectified?"

"Hmmm . . . Er, wait till you meet Halcyon," was the ominous reply.

Completely unaware of the forces that were gathering to overturn her life, Halcyon was in the woods stalking a fawn she had seen with its mother but a scant two days ago.

Scarcely bothering to lift her skirts out of the reach of snagging briers and thistles, she sped barefoot over the rough and uneven terrain, intent only on catching another glimpse of the delicate, soft-eyed creature that had stood fearlessly regarding her with innocent appraisal the last time she had stumbled upon it feeding in the underbrush.

Although dirty and disheveled at this moment because of her frantic pursuit, she was not unlike a fawn herself, with her wide green eyes and red-blond hair that framed a piquant face.

"If it is not down by the stream," she murmured

7

to herself, "I shall climb the big oak tree and see if I can glimpse it across the meadows."

She darted along the winding tracks through the trees, her tiny feet never faltering, even when they encountered sharp stones and thorns. Halcyon was used to running barefoot, carefree as the wild sylvan animals themselves as she roamed the forest and the surrounding hills.

She reached the stream and anxiously searched its winding length. Not finding what she so eagerly desired, she hoisted her skirts and nimbly crossed the stream, jumping from one protruding stone to another until she was safely across.

Having thus arrived in one piece at the old oak tree, she began a long ascent, her rough-skinned feet finding footholds in the craggy bark, whilst her hands grasped the gnarled knots above her head and pulled her up into the camouflage of the foliage. Safely ensconced in the topmost branches, she surveyed her world.

The broad blue expanse of the sky encompassed her like a dome, whilst the land stretched out far below her. Dizzily happy perched above the world like this, she giggled a little to herself. If there were any clouds, my head would be quite immersed in them! she thought.

To the west the land dropped sharply away from the woods, flattening out into prairies and meadows dotted with a profusion of wild flowers. It was here, where the grass was lush and green, that the deer were often to be seen at evening. But now the meadows were bare of animal life, save for a few scampering rabbits enjoying the warmth of the afternoon sun.

The sea of foliage beneath Halcyon gently swayed

in a light summer breeze, giving the impression of slowly undulating waters.

Twisting around in her lofty perch, she craned her neck till she could see the manor house nestling in the folds of the hills a few hundred yards to the east. How battered and dismal it looked as the glinting sun revealed the peeling timber and the crumbling stone! It was, nevertheless, a dignified-looking house; it must have been really a beautiful sight years ago in its prime.

Turning her attention in another direction, Halcyon detected the glint of a moving object speeding along the Great North Road, and she squinted her eyes till it resolved itself into a distinguishable carriage drawn by four gleaming black horses. To her surprise, it turned off the main road and began a rumbling, swaying progress along the rutted cart track that led past the manor house. No doubt it was making for the inn a few miles hence, thought Halcyon, dismissing the matter with a shrug.

Regretfully deciding that it was time to return home, she slid carelessly down to the lower branches of the oak, catching herself up abruptly when she realized that the object of her search was even now cropping the grass below her. So enchanted was she with the sight of the pale beige creature that she was unaware of the long tear in her dress, which had caught on a projecting branch, and, what was even more surprising, she did not even feel the jagged slash made by a sharp finger of bark down her leg.

She hung there, suspended in midair by her aching arms, scarcely daring to breathe for fear of frightening away the lovely fawn, until she was no longer able to sustain the strain, and with a small cry of alarm, she let go of the branch of the tree and landed in a crumpled heap beside the startled animal.

She thought afterwards it must have been too terrified to move, for, contrary to her expectations, it did not retreat, but stood surveying her, its eyes dilated into liquid pools in which she could see her own reflection.

"Don't be frightened," she whispered softly. Her breath caught in wonder as the fawn bent down and softly nuzzled her ear before stepping daintily back and springing away across the river.

It had been such a fleeting, incredible moment that Halcyon could scarcely believe it had really happened.

She stood up, then gave a sharp cry as her left leg buckled beneath her weight. In dismay she surveyed the angry weal down her leg; it was now bleeding profusely and throbbing in pain.

Once again she struggled to her feet and limped towards the river. Suddenly, a movement in the bushes caught her attention and, looking up, she saw a man on horseback calmly regarding her.

They stared at each other for several moments before he jumped nimbly from his horse, tossed the rein over the branch of a tree, and said, "You've hurt yourself!" His voice was low, smooth, and controlled, matching the fluidity of his movements as he came towards her, cautiously, much as she herself would approach a frightened fawn.

Halcyon stood looking at him, wondering vaguely whether she ought not to be afraid of an encounter with a stranger in the seclusion of the woods. Still, common sense told her that she couldn't take flight anyway, or, if she did, she would not get very far before he overtook her.

He was an impressive figure, tall and well-built, dressed in a dark brown frock coat and creamy beige breeches with a matching waistcoat. His cravat was neatly tied and his legs were encased in hessian boots. His whole figure not only was well decked out but also exuded superb physical strength. Halcyon shuddered as she realized that she would be no match for him if he were to . . .

Her gaze swiveled up to his face, fear beginning to lace her emotions as the possibilities of acute danger began to form in her mind. Her hand rose instinctively to her breast, giving the stranger an indication of her turbulent thoughts.

"Don't be afraid," he soothed. "I won't hurt you."

"W-who are you?" she stammered.

"A reasonable question." She detected amusement in his voice. "I suppose you don't see many strangers around these parts."

"Not on our land," she agreed, with some of her spirit returning.

"Touché!" An admiring glance flickered over her. "Sit down." He gave her a little push and she sank to the springy turf, and, as though mesmerized, allowed him to lift the hem of her dress and examine the cut on her leg.

Briefly Halcyon wondered whether this could be construed as an indelicacy.

"It's scarcely possible to observe the proprieties and deal effectively with a small emergency as well," said the stranger, effortlessly divining her thoughts.

His fingers were deft and gentle as he probed the wound and removed small particles of bark embedded in the torn flesh, before cupping his hand and scooping water from the river to bathe her leg.

"I know it looks nasty, and probably aches quite intolerably just now, but I fancy it's little more than a scratch." As he spoke he removed his cravat and bent over her once again to use this item as a bandage. He was immersed in his task, his head very close to hers, and Halcyon noted how his brown hair was sprinkled with golden highlights. The lines of his cheek and jaw were firm, his mouth curved slightly upward with the hint of good nature, and his eyelashes were thick and of a shade darker than his hair.

Suddenly he glanced up, and their eyes locked. He had the most amazingly clear gray eyes, piercing as the flash of a sword blade in the sunlight. Halcyon felt her breath tighten in her chest, and a flush rose to her cheeks.

As they gazed at each other, a roguish light entered his eyes and swiftly he bent and pressed his lips to hers. It was but a brief kiss, light as the touch of a butterfly, but it sent a shiver of some nameless emotion snaking through Halcyon's slender frame.

"Oh!" she cried, staring at him half in surprise, half in consternation. Then, belatedly remembering that this was scarcely the act of a gentleman, she assumed a tone of reproof. "I hardly think, sir, that such an act was necessary in the circumstances. You presume too much on such slight acquaintance, and, grateful though I may be for your timely assistance, you have taken advantage of my gratitude."

She made as if to rise to her feet, but instantly the stranger stood up and, placing his hands on either side of her waist, lifted her upright and placed her gently on her feet.

"But it was necessary, you know." He was laughing at her. "Oh, purely for medicinal purposes, I do assure you. It was meant as an antidote for pain, you see."

"Nonsense!" She must not let his charm undermine her sense of what was right and wrong.

"You mean to say it didn't work?" He pretended to be amazed. "Did it not quite drive from your mind the pain of your leg?"

He was right! She had forgotten about her injured leg. Other emotions had pushed out any thought of pain. "I—I . . ." She blushed and lowered her eyes.

"Dear me," he continued, "it bodes ill for me if you are still in pain, for I must be losing my touch." He affected to look crestfallen.

Unable to hide her amusement any longer, Halcyon burst into laughter.

"Really, sir, I should be annoyed with you, but I suspect that nobody is capable of feeling that sentiment for long as far as you are concerned."

"I thank you, kind lady"—he bowed exaggeratedly low—"for restoring my faith in myself."

He was like no one she had ever known. Not, of course, that her experience was very extensive. She was standing beside him by the edge of the stream, and she realized now as she craned her neck to look up at him, just how tall he was. He must be at least six feet—tall, even for a man.

She longed to prolong her acquaintance of him, but he had finished bandaging her leg, his horse was becoming restive as it stood in the shelter of the trees, and she herself was late for dinner.

"I—I bid you good day, sir. And, thank you!"

She prepared to make her way back across the river, lifting her skirts out of the way of the rushing water.

"Wait!" he cried. "Let me assist you home, at least."

He untethered his horse and quickly mounted. "Come." He pointed to the space in front of him. "Give me your hand."

"Oh, I couldn't . . ." Her voice trailed away as her traitorous feet carried her towards him. She felt herself swung upwards and spun around, and without quite knowing how it had happened, she found herself perched in front of the stranger.

"In which direction do you live?" His arms tightened around her.

"Across the clearing." She pointed. "And follow that path that leads through the trees. The manor house is a few hundred yards beyond."

She felt him stiffen.

"The manor house? You are from the manor?"

"Yes." Was she imagining it, or did his voice sound constrained, distant?

"And you are . . . ?"

"Lucius Glaybourne's daughter . . . Do you know my father?"

"Slightly . . . I believe I met him once . . . many years ago."

"Then perhaps you would like to come in and renew your acquaintance? I'm sure—"

"Thank you, no! I mean . . . perhaps another time."

They had arrived at the side entrance to the manor. The stranger silently helped her to dismount.

14

Glancing fleetingly up at him, Halcyon thought that he really was a stranger now; he was no longer the charming, friendly man who had wound his cravat around her injured leg and laughingly stolen a kiss.

For some reason he had suddenly changed his mind about her. He had liked her before, she was sure of it—and now he was regarding her disdainfully down his long aristocratic nose.

She turned away, annoyed. She hadn't asked for his help or a ride back to the manor. And she was late for dinner. She had no time for ill-mannered strangers of uncertain humor.

"G-goodbye . . . and thank you again . . . Oh! Your cravat! . . . Mayhap I can return it to you when it is laundered?"

He watched her limping progress to the door, and as she turned and looked at him, regretting that, after all, she would probably never meet him again, she saw a burning flicker that came to his eyes and disappeared again so quickly that she could not be certain she had not merely imagined it.

"Keep the cravat," he told her, "as a reminder . . . of . . . not to climb trees. Next time I may not be there to help you."

He wheeled his horse around and was gone before Halcyon could think of a suitable reply.

She was flushed and disheveled, but happy, as she made her way to her father's library.

"Papa! You'll never guess what happened today!" she cried out as she burst into the room. Then she stopped, confused, as she saw the stranger seated by the window. Belatedly she became aware of her appearance, her torn dress and dirty, mudstained feet, the scratches on her hands where the rough bark of

15

the oak tree had caught them, and the unkempt state of her hair. She backed out of the room with a muttered apology and raced up to her room with scarcely a backward glance at the astonished woman who gaped at her retreating back.

"Well, really, Lucius!" Lady Hensham threw up her hands in horror and sprang agitatedly to her feet. "Oh, my goodness! What atrocity is this, Lucius? You have brought up the child to be worse than a hoyden—why, she is little better than a *savage!*" Lady Hensham swayed unsteadily on her feet, her emotions threatening to overcome her as she staggered back, groping for the security of her chair. "Oooh! How ever am I going to explain all this to the marquis?"

Vaguely aware that Lady Henshaw had received something in the nature of a shock, and from his dim recollection of women and their delicate ways deducing that his cousin was about to have an attack of the vapors, Lucius Glaybourne jumped forward to assist her. But she was of stronger mettle than he had realized; she brushed him away with scarcely disguised irritation.

"Do stop fussing, Lucius! My constitution is equal to this and any other setback, however serious, I do assure you!" She fumbled in her reticule and pulled out a fan with which she beat the air around her whilst pressing to her nose a lace handkerchief, heavily impregnated with perfume. "But mark my words, the marquis will not be pleased with this nonsense."

"My dear cousin, pray do not take on so," protested Lucius. "The situation is not as bad as you would have it. Although I must plead guilty to allowing my

16

daughter far too slack a rein, I nevertheless can guarantee that she has been brought up as a lady."

"Hmph! I saw scant proof of that," sniffed her ladyship. "Rushing in here like a revolting peasant! Where are your senses, Lucius? I do declare your brains have become addled with living too long alone."

"But I'm not alone, don't you know. Halcyon and I have been much together, and, believe me, although her upbringing and her education have not been exactly . . . conventional, she has received a liberal amount of both."

"Of what education do you speak, cousin?" Lady Hensham brightened up a little, as she thought Halcyon's father was about to reassure her on this point. "You mean to say that she has had governesses?"

"No-o . . . Not exactly."

"Do not play games with me, Lucius! Either she has or she has not been in the care of a governess. What then is this *not exactly*?"

"Ah, Henrietta! She has been an old man's delight," murmured Lucius with a catch in his throat. "I can't tell you the happy hours we have spent together, the talks we have enjoyed, the way we have pondered over the wonders of this world. I have educated her myself, and I flatter myself that her brain is equal to that of any man schooled in the most exclusive of institutions."

"A lot of good that will do her," was Lady Hensham's waspish reply. "You think that the men will swarm around her like bees around a honey-pot because of her brain? And I beg you to remember that it is not for an old man's delight that she should be schooled, but to become the wife of the marquis's son. Was that not the agreement you made with your friend of long standing?"

"Indeed it was. And I would not go against my word."

"It is unfortunate you did not prepare the girl, though. Perhaps then she would have been more mindful of the more feminine pursuits of life. Oh, what a tangle is all this. You realize, Lucius, that she just won't do as she is. I shall have to work on her manners and her deportment—not to mention her *dreadful* appearance—before we can present her to the marquis as his son's prospective bride."

"You are not suggesting, by any chance, that she is not good enough for him, are you?" asked Lucius in a deceptively mild voice.

"Indeed no! What ever gave you that impression?" Lady Hensham was acute enough to detect the note of menace in her cousin's voice, and, feeling that she might well have been a little harsh in her judgment and condemnation, she hastened to add, "Why, I do think I myself could be very slightly to blame in this matter. I should have known when her poor dear mother died that a widower's household was no place for a young lady's upbringing. As her godmother, I had a moral obligation to see that she was well cared for."

"I *have* cared for her, Henrietta."

"Of course you have, but you have scarcely catered to her femininity. You know I would have taken her with me to Europe if it had been at all possible, Lucius, but as you are well aware, the life of a military man's wife is not an easy one."

"I know that, cousin, rest assured of that."

"However—" Lady Hensham squared her shoulders as one accepting a great burden. "—now that poor, dear Marmaduke is dead, I can devote myself entirely to the task of preparing Halcyon for the role she is to assume in life."

"You are too kind," murmured Lucius somewhat dryly.

"Not at all." Lady Hensham graciously accepted the praise as her due. "But now it rests with you to break the news to Halcyon." She stood up, replaced her gloves, and prepared to depart.

"Won't you stay for dinner, cousin?"

"Such *had* been my intention. However, circumstances would appear to dictate otherwise. No, dear Lucius, I think you should acquaint Halcyon with her prospects for the future in private. I shall return tomorrow."

CHAPTER TWO

"No, Papa! Say it isn't so! Tell me that this is just some terrible dream!"

Halcyon stared at her father in dismay, her eyes wide and frightened at the news he had just imparted.

"It is true, my dear. You know I would never speak falsely in such a matter." Lucius's voice was regretful but firm.

"Then why have you surprised me with this news, Papa? Oh, I thought you were not just my father, but even more, a friend. How can it be that you have misled me in this cruel manner? I trusted you—" Her voice broke off as a sob invaded her throat and prevented further speech.

"Then please still trust me, I beg of you, daughter. This marriage was arranged many years ago when your poor, dear mother was yet alive. The Marquis of Rexdale's son is a very eligible man, sought after by many young ladies of quality. Why, it is said that he could have his pick of any one of the titled ladies that frequent the Court."

"Then why, pray, does he not choose one of them?"

"He is promised to you."

"A promise that I shall scarce hold him to."

"Nevertheless, it must be so."

"But why? Why?"

Lucius Glaybourne realized that his daughter deserved a full explanation. She had been a dear and animated companion to him, and he found it difficult to look upon her solely as his daughter and one who must now do his bidding, however unwilling she might be or however unpalatable she might find it.

He sighed and sank back into his chair, carefully taking a pinch of snuff before beginning his story.

"It all seems so long ago—another era; no, more than that, another lifetime. Perhaps that is why I didn't tell you. I had almost forgotten my promise until your godmother came this afternoon and reminded me that it must be kept."

"Another surprise," murmured Halcyon. "I did not realize that I had a godmother!"

"She has been much in foreign parts with her husband. You knew her as a child, but mayhap you have forgotten those brief meetings."

"And how does she enter these unfortunate circumstances?"

"Only as one who was acquainted with the arrangement made at that time. You see, my dear, I had a very staunch friend and ally, the Marquis of Rexdale. We spent much time in each other's company. I was not always a recluse, you see, Halcyon." Her father briefly smiled. "His wife was dead and he had just one child, a son and heir. Well, to be brief, for I am aware that you are impatient of the details, I saved his life in a city brawl. He professed himself eternally grateful, and ever sought to repay me in some significant way."

Lucius Glaybourne stared into the dark fold of the velvet curtains, his memory lost in the mists of the past. As the silence lengthened, Halcyon gently prodded him.

"Well?"

Her father roused himself with an effort.

"Your mother was dying. We knew that. Her prime concern was for you, and the difficulty I should have raising you alone, and, when the time came, finding a suitable match for you."

"And that's where the marquis came in."

"Yes. He pledged his word that his son should marry my little daughter when she reached the age of seventeen. Your mother's fears were allayed—she died shortly thereafter, secure in the knowledge that you would be well provided for."

"But she need not have worried. I am not some pale milk-and-white miss who needs help to survive with dignity in this world."

"Agreed," said her father with some amusement. "But at that time, we did not know that you would grow into such a beautiful and charming young daughter."

"Then—" Halcyon's eyes brightened, "there is no need for such an agreement to be kept, is there? I do not need the protection of an arranged marriage, and I am sure that the Marquis of Rexdale will echo my sentiments wholeheartedly."

"I'm afraid it's not quite as simple as that."

"What do you mean? Why not?"

"One cannot renege on a promise."

"One can if both parties agree . . ."

"And how is your mother to agree from beyond the grave?"

"Oh!"

"You see? The promise must be kept."

23

"But—the marquis's son . . . the one to whom I am promised . . ."

"Was of age at the time and perfectly willing to comply with his father's wishes."

"B-but how could he be? Why, he did not even know me, and in any case I was just a child at the time. For all he knew I might grow up squint-eyed and buck-toothed!"

"Exactly! Which only does him all the more credit. He loved his father—as he still does now—and jealously guards his honor."

Did Halcyon detect a note of reproof in her father's voice? She glanced at him quickly, but he was gazing at her with his usual mild and affectionate expression.

"And—and you would have me protect your honor in the same way?" she asked bitterly.

"I should like it," he agreed.

"But, Papa!" Halcyon jumped up, all her agitation returning with a rush, as she realized that she was bound into this more securely that she had imagined, by circumstances beyond her control. "What of *love?* I thought to marry a man I loved."

"Love?" Lucius Glaybourne pondered this new idea for a long time. Love? He gazed at his daughter in puzzlement. This was something that he had omitted to take into account. He was a man—kindhearted, but realistic and unromantic. Where on earth did women get the idea that love was a prerequisite to marriage? Love—an illusive commodity at the best of times; one was lucky if it developed later in the marriage.

He had spent so much of his time with Halcyon that he tended to look upon her as a very intelligent

24

human being, but one not belonging to any sex. He realized now his error. He had made his plans; he had let explanations and preparations go by the board, so sure had he been that Halcyon would accept this match with true manly stoicism. But love! He hadn't bargained for that.

"Is love so very important?" he asked now.

"Of course it is!" cried Halcyon. Oh, how blind, how unfeeling men were! It was expressly this lack of sentiment in most of them that had made her determined to choose her own mate with care, making sure that he was possessed of a romantic and deeply caring heart underneath his firm exterior. "Were not you and mother in love?"

"No. That was something that grew after marriage . . . and very lucky we considered ourselves, too."

"And you would deprive me of that?"

"Halcyon!" cried her father in exasperation. "I would deprive you of nothing! The Marquis of Rexdale's son is brave, honest, and an exquisitely turned-out gentleman. You could do far worse."

"Can you promise me that I shall love him—and he will love me?" she demanded.

"No." His voice was sad. "You know I can't do that. But it is a good match, nevertheless."

"If I choose to accept it," she reminded him.

"You—you will, won't you?" Surely she would not dare to refuse. He would be the laughingstock of all England—not to mention how the Marquis of Rexdale would feel.

Halcyon was aware, even as she withheld her acquiescence, that she flaunted an empty power. She really had no choice. She was bound to her father's word. If she disobeyed him now, it would be the

25

certain end of their camaraderie and friendship, something far surpassing a father-and-daughter relationship.

Her feet trod lightly over the threadbare carpet as she approached him. Then she knelt down on the floor beside him and rested her head in his lap as she had done so many times since she was a child.

"Y-yes, Papa," she choked. "I will accept." Then she burst into tears.

"At least the girl has some idea of daughterly duty," was Lady Hensham's comment when she heard the story from Lucius the following day.

True to her word, she had returned in her landau and was now once again in the library with her cousin. She was in an infinitely better mood today, having passed a very comfortable night in one of the best inns in Britain.

Now that she was refreshed and relaxed after her tiresomely long journey, most of her habitual good humor had returned to her.

"Halcyon is a good child," affirmed Lucius.

"Woman," corrected Lady Hensham reprovingly. "Lucius, I am convinced that half the trouble has been that Halcyon has already entered into womanhood without being in the slightest bit aware of the implications of such a state."

"I have prepared her very badly." He had the grace to look shamefaced.

"You have prepared her not at all!"

"The thing I feel so badly about, Henrietta, is the way she cried so bitterly after she had agreed to my wishes . . . some nonsense about love. You women are the most unpredictable of creatures, I do declare!

I could have sworn that Halcyon had a good, steady, no-nonsense type of head on her shoulders."

"And she proved you wrong." Lady Hensham was smiling now. "And, Lucius, what do you mean about love being nonsense? It is the very staff and pivot of life itself. What else do you suppose makes the world go round?"

"Egad!" Lucius Glaybourne blinked at his cousin in disbelief. "You too?" he muttered.

"Why not?" Lady Hensham ruffled her feathers in annoyance. "Why not me too?" It always annoyed her to think what blind creatures men were. They couldn't see past her stern, forbidding exterior to the mellowness within. "Pah!" she said. "Men!"

She was silent for fully five minutes whilst she considered Lucius's latest piece of information.

"So the child wants to fall in love, does she?" she murmured half to herself.

"That's what she said. I am sorry to have made such a muddle of everything for her."

"I think not," declared her ladyship.

Lucius looked at her sharply. "What do you mean?" he asked.

"You haven't spoilt anything at all for her. In fact, an idea comes to me just now that may possibly save the day and leave all of us very happy." A small, contented smile was playing around her lips. "Listen to me . . . As you are aware, I have stated that Halcyon is not quite ready to meet her prospective husband just yet. I shall take her under my wing, teach the airs and pastimes of a lady to her, and allow her to meet and mix with the high society in Bath."

"You would enjoy that, I know," agreed Lucius, "but it seems to me that such freedom and excitement in an environment where she will meet many eligible beaux will only compound our problem, my dear cousin."

"Did you tell Halcyon the name of her future husband?"

"I believe I did mention the Marquis of Rexdale's son."

"Excellent! Excellent!" Lady Hensham was positively beaming.

"But—but, Henrietta, have you considered what will happen if Halcyon falls in love in Bath?"

Lady Hensham fluttered her fan and laughted delightedly. "My dear Lucius, that's precisely what I am counting on!"

CHAPTER THREE

Lady Hensham's landau was excessively well appointed. The exterior was shiny and black; an elaborate and colorful crest was painted on the side. Inside, the padded black leather seats afforded much comfort to the traveler.

Halcyon was aware that such a rig would cost a great deal of money, and she regarded Lady Hensham with curiosity as they commenced their journey. Her husband must have been a very wealthy man to have left his widow in such fortunate straits.

Not that money and ostentatious wealth impressed her unduly, but she could not help but be mindful of how much her father's life was restricted by lack of this commodity.

She craned her head forward to catch a last glimpse of the manor house, the only home she had ever known, before the coach turned on to the main road. How dilapidated and forlorn it looked! How different it would have looked had her father, just once in his life, been possessed of adequate funds.

Finally the manor was lost to view, and Halcyon settled back on the springy leather, closing her eyes to block the tears that suddenly threatened.

"Don't worry, child. Your father will be all right," Lady Hensham assured her with amazing perspicacity.

"I hate to leave him alone." Halcyon's eyes softened as she thought of the many happy hours they had spent together.

"He won't be alone. He has his books. And don't flatter yourself," added Lady Hensham brusquely, feeling that too great a sympathy at this time would only serve to make Halcyon more depressed, "that you won't be forgotten the minute he buries his nose in one of those dusty tomes of his."

"You're right." Halcyon sighed. Her father had ever been one who lived in the world of his books. It was a world that he had encouraged her to share with him, and she knew she would always look back on her childhood as a very special time.

But there was much more to life than books. Halcyon knew that. Much as she had enjoyed her father's dissertations on the ancient world, she had not been as wholeheartedly committed to the pursuit of knowledge of ancient times as her enthusiastic parent.

She longed to experience life—sometimes with a longing so intense that it hurt her deep inside. Her life hitherto had been curiously devoid of contact with others; she had lived a lonely life with her father, who was such a recluse that he did not encourage visitors.

Now, at last, it seemed that Halcyon's world was opening up, like a bud newly come to bloom. Eager, excited anticipation rose within her breast, and she turned to Lady Hensham, a thousand questions on her lips.

"Do you think the marquis's son will mind?" she asked breathlessly.

"Mind what?"

"The fact that I will not be presented to him till later in the year."

Her godmother nodded complacently. "Leave everything to me, my dear. I am sure that, approached in the proper way, he will see nothing but good in this delay."

"I suppose that if he were to see me now, he would throw up his hands in horror," continued Halcyon, mindful of her godmother's reaction to her appearance the first time they had met.

Lady Hensham allowed her eyes to take critical stock of her charge. "Well, I must say that you are much improved from that dreadful hoyden who came rushing like a whirlwind into her father's library."

Halcyon laughed outright at the memory. "I must have given you quite a shock. I had no idea Papa had a visitor—such an event was a most unusual occurrence in our house."

"I was all but ready to turn tail and forget my duty as your godmother, child," said Lady Hensham, her smile softening her words. "But already you have more of the semblance of a lady."

"Thanks to your kindness—and the consummate skill of your abigail, Godmother."

Lady Hensham turned to the third person in the landau, a quiet, docile young woman with a very shy demeanor. "Yes, indeed, Emily, you have worked wonders with Miss Halcyon."

"Thank you, m'lady."

"Positive miracles," underlined Halcyon, her eyes bright with admiration as she recalled how the self-effacing Emily had set to work with deft hands and transformed a tangled mop of unruly red hair into a

31

shining, elegant coiffure, with each gleaming curl pinned into place.

"Now, if we could do something about your wardrobe!"

"It is dreadful, isn't it?" said Halcyon ruefully as she surveyed her worn and unfashionable clothes. "I'm afraid that father was never much interested in fashion, you know. And as we very rarely went to town, I was not exactly cognizant of the latest mode."

"We shall rectify that upon arrival in London. I intend to spend a few days there so that something may speedily be done about your dress." Lady Hensham regarded her goddaughter with practiced eyes; with her quite startling coloring, the glory of her hair, the smooth peach-bloom of her skin, the blazing emerald of her eyes, she was going to take many a man's heart by storm.

Upon meeting Halcyon for the second time, in a rather cleaner, tidier state, Lady Hensham had seen at once the distinct possibilities that the girl possessed.

Her young figure, almost sylphlike, was just now blooming into womanhood. She had a natural poise and dignity of manner that had not been at first apparent, and her clear and musical voice had none of the grating harshness that too often spoilt a woman's beauty.

Contrary to her first strangled assertions to the opposite, Lady Hensham had the growing conviction that the son of the Marquis of Rexdale was going to be quite overwhelmingly delighted with his prospective bride.

With complacent satisfaction, she settled back in

her seat, and prepared to suffer the long journey from Solchester to London. The swaying of the carriage soon caused her eyelids to flutter and then drop as she fell asleep.

Halcyon was far too excited to follow her example. They were passing through a landscape that was green and only slightly undulating. The road wound through meadows and farmland, occasionally passing through a small cluster of houses or cottages. If this had been a public coach, Halcyon surmised, they would have made a brief stop at the inns to allow passengers to embark or disembark.

Towards noon, when the sun was riding high in the sky, they stopped at a country inn, and descended to partake of a lunch that would appease their hunger till dinnertime.

"We'll be in London in time for dinner," Lady Hensham assured her two traveling companions as she lifted her skirts elegantly to step from the landau. "Oh, how I do hate these tedious journeys," she added, totally oblivious of the fact that she, as a rich lady owning her own means of luxurious transportation, traveled with far less inconvenience than the common folk.

"I think it's all so exciting! I don't mind it at all," ventured Halcyon, though even she was sore and weary by the end of the day, and longing for a cessation of the swaying and jumping of the coach.

Her spirits revived, however, as they reached the outskirts of London. The pot-holed, rutted road that fell away at the edges to a veritable quagmire, now grew wider. Soon they were within the city where the coach rumbled noisily over the cobbled streets and clattered through the dark and narrow alleys where the houses were huddled together in the sinister half-light.

The streets were dirty. The noise of the people, the coaches, the drays, and the beggars rose to an unbearable crescendo.

Halcyon pressed her nose to the window, trying to take in everything at once. So this was the fabled London about which she had heard so much!

On both sides of the street rose tall houses with plate-glass windows. The lower floors of these seemed to consist mainly of shops with glass fronts, behind which a thousand candles lit up the silverware, engravings, paintings, books, as well as pewter and glass, clocks and precious stones. There was women's finery decked in display and countless treasures that made Halcyon gasp in delight.

The streets were lit as though for a festival; in the windows of the apothecaries and druggists blazed phials and bottles of colored glass that shot forth a myriad of rainbow lights.

In the middle of the streets rolled carriages and chaises, with all manner of humanity filling the pavements and spilling out on to the roads, darting between the wheels of the thundering coaches. The mob and rabble called noisily to each other and they pushed and shoved and jostled.

"I've never seen so many people in my life!" Halcyon exclaimed. "Nor did I imagine there were so many people in the whole of England, even!"

"Ugh! What a horrible seething mass, I do declare," was Lady Hensham's comment. "These streets are not the place for a lady, Halcyon, and I hope that you will remember that. The outskirts of the city are where thieves, beggars, and cutthroats

34

abound, and it would be taking one's life into one's own hands to rub shoulders with these crowds." She shuddered delicately, and pressed her perfumed handkerchief to her nose to block the pungent smell of the streets.

Finally the landau managed to plow its way through the people, and soon they were in wider, more fashionable streets where there was far less evidence of the bustling rabble.

Lady Hensham breathed a sigh of relief.

"My brother and his wife are expecting us. It is in their house in Grosvenor Square that we shall be spending a few days before traveling on further to my house in Bath."

"I have heard that the houses in Grosvenor Square are very beautiful," ventured Halcyon.

A nod came from her ladyship.

"Perhaps you have heard of Sir Henry Cecil? He was ambassador to Tuscany for many years."

Halcyon had to admit her ignorance. Her knowledge of present-day facts was sadly lacking.

"Hmm. I expect you would have heard of him if he'd been an Ancient Greek" was her godmother's somewhat caustic comment. "Well, never mind. Here we are at last."

The coach halted and her ladyship showed more animation than she had throughout the journey.

The door of Number 6 Grosvenor Square was thrown open, and a butler and a maid stood on the threshold.

Halcyon had an impression of a large entrance hall, velvet upholstery, many sparkling lights, and a grand staircase leading to the upper floors.

They were ushered into the drawing room, where

Sir Henry, his wife, and two daughters were awaiting them.

"So sorry to be late, my dears," called Lady Hensham, as she sailed into the room like a grand duchess. "You wouldn't believe the dreadful state of the roads today. How are you, my dear Henry? And you, Millicent? My dear, what a splendid gown."

"We delayed dinner for you, Henrietta . . . And this is your goddaughter—Lucius's child." Lady Cecil turned to her husband, "Oh, do you not see the resemblance to her mother, Henry?"

"Indeed I do." Sir Henry's eyes held a warm glow. "Save that your beauty, Miss Glaybourne, surpasses even hers."

Whilst Halcyon blushed furiously at this, not knowing how to answer, her godmother intervened.

"Don't fill the child's head with vain thoughts, Henry. Besides, as you can see, compliments only serve to confuse her. A more naïve and guileless young miss I have yet to meet." Then, turning to Halcyon, she said, "Come, child, let us freshen ourselves before dinner—with all haste possible, for we have already kept these good people waiting far too long."

"You are in your usual room, Henrietta," said her sister-in-law, ringing for the maid.

"Mama, may we accompany Miss Glaybourne to her room?" asked the two daughters, almost in unison.

"Why, yes, if she has no objection."

Halcyon professed that she had none, and all three of them made their way up the elegant staircase to a small room at the side of the house.

The two girls were disposed to be friendly. "Mayhap you would like me to send my abigail to you?" suggested Elizabeth, the tall blond one, who was quite definitely the elder of the two.

Halcyon shyly refused, declaring that Lady Hensham's Emily would see to her few needs.

"You're right between the two of us," smiled Jane, who, with her dark curls, her pink-and-white complexion, and her tiny figure, was just like a Dresden doll. "Elizabeth's room is here, to the left, and I am right on the other side. And your godmother's room is just down that corridor—that blue door on the right."

Halcyon's room was small, though elegantly furnished with delicate Chippendale furniture, and carpet and curtains of pale eggshell blue.

"Now," said Jane, perching herself on the edge of the bed, "do tell us all about yourself. Elizabeth and I have been perfectly dying to meet you."

"Not now, Jane," her sister admonished, flashing a rueful smile at Halcyon. "Let our guest refresh herself first. And then, as I am sure you are mindful, dinner is about to be served."

"I won't delay," promised Halcyon, as the other two prepared to leave. "H-how shall I find my way to the dining room when I am ready?"

"We'll be back directly," Elizabeth assured her. "Wait till we come."

Someone had brought Halcyon's bags up to her room. With dismay she surveyed her pitifully scant wardrobe. It had not missed her attention how elegantly and expensively attired were Lady Cecil and her daughters. They were very much in the *mode*, whereas her gowns . . . She sighed. It couldn't be helped. At least godmother had promised to fit her out without delay.

She was ready when Elizabeth and Jane returned for her. They once more led the way, taking her down the wide staircase and across the hall to another room where a sumptuous repast was laid out. Everyone else was already assembled.

"I do hope I did not delay everyone," murmured Halcyon as they all took their places at the shining Chippendale table.

"Indeed you didn't," Lady Cecil assured her. "Your godmother herself came down but a few seconds before you did."

Rather miserably conscious that her dress did not live up to the lavish attire of the others at the table, Halcyon tried not to feel too gauche. She fumbled with the front of her bodice and tried to pull down out of sight the somewhat worn skirt of her gown.

"Don't fidget so, child," her godmother told her. "Your dress will do very nicely for now—although not in the best of mode." Lady Hensham was well aware of what was troubling her charge. "Halcyon and I shall be going straightway to the dressmaker's in the morning," she told the company at large. "I'm afraid her wardrobe has been sadly neglected of late."

"But one does not need too much in the country, I'm sure," said Lady Cecil kindly, "particularly if one does not entertain on a very lavish scale."

"We entertained not at all," Halcyon informed her. "Papa always said that he had neither the stomach nor the funds for company."

"Halcyon," reproved Lady Hensham, fearing that her goddaughter might come out with some revela-

38

tions that would not be flattering to herself. "I fear you had better not quote your dear papa too accurately on occasion."

Halcyon was puzzled. "You mean I should not speak of being poor? Is it a sin in the eyes of society to be poor? Because, if so—"

"Nay, do not distress yourself so, dear Miss Glaybourne," Sir Henry quickly interposed. "You are among family and friends now, and may thus speak your mind. I admit that our society places an undue emphasis on wealth—so much so that it is considered indelicate to refer to one's lack of it. Be that as it may, we all know your father as a gentleman and a friend. The fact that his estate has fallen on hard times does not lessen him in our estimation."

"You know my father, then?" asked Halcyon in astonishment. It occurred to her that she had seen none of these people in her father's house within the last ten years, and yet they all claimed his acquaintance.

"My dear child," Lady Millicent smiled across the table at her, "your father was not always a recluse, you know."

"So he told me, though I must confess that I never knew him otherwise."

"Since your mother died he has been so. But in former years, he and your mother entertained quite often and were regularly seen together at the theatre or the opera in London."

Halcyon's brow furrowed in puzzlement. "I was not aware that my father was ever able to live in such a way. How his circumstances must have changed." Her father had never spoken to her about his finances; such matters were a closed book to her. But

39

she knew that there had never been much money to spare. Although mostly lost in his love of the past, the harsh realities of modern-day living had sometimes penetrated his awareness, and on such occasions he had muttered about "the dashed expense of everything" before losing himself in his books once again.

"It is painfully apparent to all of us," said Lady Hensham, putting down her fork and daintily wiping her mouth with her serviette, "that your father has left you lamentably in ignorance of certain facts with which you should be familiar. What do you say, Millicent? Henry?"

The other two nodded their agreement.

"Your mother came of an extremely good family. She was, in fact, a cousin to the old Marquis of Rexdale. Although bearing no title herself, she did come to your father with a considerable dowry. An honorable man, an erudite scholar, your father nevertheless was never worldly enough to acquire financial success. No, child—" Lady Hensham held up a cautionary hand as she saw that Halcyon would have protested at this harsh comment on her parent. "It has to be said, although without any censure on our part. Good heavens! It was because he was so innocently unworldly that your dear mother loved him so. She used to say that a better, more amiable man never walked the face of this earth. But I digress. Your mother's yearly income, settled on her by her father, died with her, and that was when your father's financial troubles began. Such a silly thing that her money should not then have passed to you, child."

"I wish it could have done," said Halcyon slowly,

thinking how different their lives would have been with just a little more money. Oh, she never had supposed that money made happiness, but there had been times when the supply of food in the house had been dismally low, and the large, half-empty rooms of the manor had swirled with drafts from the broken windows. "But why on earth did my father continue to try to keep up the manor? Why did we not move to a smaller place?"

"The manor was your mother's birthplace," explained Sir Henry. "As such, it represented to your father, I feel sure, the only tangible link with your mother that remained to him—besides yourself, that is."

"It seems uncharacteristically romantic of him," was Halcyon's comment.

"To you, it may seem so. You should have known your father in the days when your mother was alive. He was ever quiet and subdued, I grant you that, but he was possessed of a sharp wit and a love of life that has since disappeared."

"And what will he do now that I, too, have left him?" cried Halcyon in concern.

"He will survive very well, have no fear of that. And when you are married to the Marquis of Rexdale's son, you may have your father with you in Rexdale Castle."

"You think so? What, pray, will the marquis's son think of that?" asked Halcyon a trifle bitterly. "Is it not bad enough that he has to marry a little nobody whom he has never met, a dowdy little mouse who is totally ignorant of all the social graces, let alone take in her absentminded old father?" She felt tears threatening very near. Suddenly it seemed to her that this marriage was bound to be doomed from the start, for, much as she felt that she had been unfairly pushed into it, much as she regretted that she would never be able to marry the man of her choice, and therefore perhaps never know true love, it seemed to her that the marquis's son was also getting a very rough deal.

She kept her eyes downcast, toyed with the food on her plate, and prayed that the others would not see the glistening pearls that escaped her eyelids.

"The child is tired and overwrought. Undoubtedly bed would be the best place for her. Millicent, dear, will you ring for my abigail?—I think we will both retire."

CHAPTER FOUR

Alone in her room, Halcyon was ashamed of her outburst. It was unlike her to let her emotions run away with her, and totally out of character for her to be despondent.

She concluded that the last few days, with their attendant surprises and sorrows, had been too much for her.

First there had been the shock of finding out that she was soon to be betrothed to a marquis, then the wrench of saying goodbye to her father, her dearest lifelong companion, followed by a confusion of new acquaintances, new sights, and a long and tiresome journey.

Enough emotional upheaval to dismay even the most stalwart of spirits. She had learned, too, details of her father's life that had surprised her. It was strange to think of him as a young man, deeply in love with his wife. Had her death been the blow that had driven him to live the isolated life of a recluse? How he must have loved her! Halcyon could only hope that she herself would in time love the man she was forced to marry.

What would it be like, she wondered as she climbed into bed, to be married, to share the intimate details of her life with another human being?

A thousand curious questions tormented her brain. What was Rexdale's son like? He was said to be very presentable. That being the case, surely, even if she did not love him, she would not find his touch distasteful or repulsive.

She knew—had she not found out a day or two ago?—that she was not averse to being kissed. She blushed at the memory, feeling that it was somehow indelicate to allow herself to recall the surprising events of that day. But in truth, she had been fiercely trying to push to the back of her mind the disturbing memory of the stranger she had encountered in the woods near the manor house. Try as she might, she could not banish him from her thoughts.

What had he been doing on their land? Who was he? He professed to know her father, but he had been disinclined to renew that acquaintance.

How kind he had been to her, bathing and bandaging her leg with his own snowy white cravat. She knew instinctively that he was a gentleman; his clothes, his bearing proclaimed that—which made it all the more surprising that he had snatched a kiss from her unsuspecting lips. One did not treat a lady in such a reprehensible manner! A serving girl, perhaps, but surely not a young lady of breeding.

The unwelcome thought came to her that perhaps that was what he had mistaken her for, a serving girl. A girl from the manor kitchens. No wonder he had changed his tune when she had introduced herself as Lucius Glaybourne's daughter!

Yes, the more she thought about it, the more certain she felt that this was what had happened. What a shock for him! Still, one could not blame him for a very natural mistake. Halcyon well knew that her dress, her untidy state after running wild through the

44

woods, had done nothing to prepare him for her identity.

She smiled to herself in secret delight as she remembered the white cravat, carefully laundered and now snowy white once more, that even now reposed in her valise. He had told her to keep it as a reminder of . . . not to climb trees! But to her, it was a reminder of much more than that. Just thinking of it brought flooding back acutely vivid memories of his gentle hands removing the slivers of bark from her wounded leg, the crisp brown hair so close that she could have reached out and touched it, the clear gray mocking eyes that had pierced her soul with a shaft of steel . . .

As Halcyon drifted off into sleep, she felt again the fleeting warmth of his kiss.

Halcyon awoke to the strangely discordant sounds of a London morning. She forced herself to lie for a few moments, savoring the knowledge that a new world was opening up before her; then, unable to bear further inaction, she jumped out of bed and ran in her nightclothes to her godmother's room.

"My dear! My dear! What's this all about?" cried that lady, hastening to gather herself together and make herself presentable for early morning scrutiny. "What ever has happened?" she asked, fancying that at the very least the house was on fire.

"Nothing is the matter, Godmother," Halcyon assured her. "Nothing except that it's morning and already the sounds of London can be heard in the streets! Oh, please may we go out early, Godmother?"

"Halcyon," reproved Lady Hensham, "one of the

first lessons you must learn is that a lady does not burst into another's room so early in the day without first ascertaining that she is expected."

"Sorry, Godmother." Halcyon's eyes were downcast, but her spirit was unrepentant. What silly rules society dictated!

"And furthermore"—her ladyship was unrelenting—"one does not—*positively* not—wander about at large in such a scanty and unseemly state of undress."

A thousand protests rose to Halcyon's lips, but she wisely bit them back, merely whispering a modest, "No, Godmother." Then her enthusiasm again got the better of her, and she sat down on the edge of Lady Hensham's bed and entreated her, "But, please, do say that we may walk out early today. Oh, I'm so looking forward to everything." She jumped up and whirled around the room, humming "London Bridge Is Falling Down."

In spite of herself, Lady Hensham could not fail to be infected by her goddaughter's good humor. Soon she was smiling too, and for the first time since the death of her husband, she felt she had something to look forward to in life.

"Come over here, child." She patted the bed beside her. "Now," she commenced as soon as Halcyon had complied with her command, "I know you think I'm an old fuddy-duddy. And you may be right." She permitted herself a small smile. "But that's not to say that I'm too old to remember what it was to be young and full of the joy of life, full of expectation for the future, and full of a scornful rejection of all the impositions of age, wisdom, and experience. Ah yes, my child." She nodded wisely at Halcyon. "I too was

46

once young enough and wild enough to want to kick against the dictates of my elders and betters, and to seek my own destiny in my own way. A nice thought . . . But it doesn't, of course, work like that. Life cannot be lived solely for oneself. There are so many other factors and considerations that crowd in on us and influence our final decisions.

"I know how you feel about this arranged marriage, my dear. Your father was most upset that you wanted so desperately to be allowed to choose for yourself. Of course, I told him that much of the culpability was his. He should have warned you many summers ago that you were destined to become the wife of the Marquis of Rexdale's son.

"You must believe that everything will work out for the best. Very often the most terrible disasters in our minds turn out to be our greatest blessings. Your father, you must remember, was only doing what he felt was right for you when he arranged this marriage years ago."

For Lady Hensham to unbend so far as to tell her all these things was no surprise to Halcyon. She had quickly seen through her godmother's stern exterior to the kind soul within. "You don't need to tell me all this, Godmother," she protested, "I am truly mindful of my duty as a daughter, and, apart from that, I am also quite resigned to marrying the Marquis of Rexdale's son. They tell me that he is very well received at Court. Such a man cannot be too bad, I tell myself. But, Godmother, the time is flying; I must back to my room."

Lady Hensham nodded. "I will send my abigail to you in half an hour."

Back in her room Halcyon walked over to the

47

window and drew back the eggshell-blue curtains. Daylight flooded in, sending a shaft of shimmering gold across the carpet.

Leaning forward to look outside, she gained the impression that the whole of London was awake and in the streets. Enticed by the warmth of the sunlight and the alluring sights below, she pulled up the sash window and leaned out over the sill, whereupon the sounds and cries of London burst upon her ears.

At the far end of the street a milkmaid cried out her wares in such a high-pitched voice that it carried clearly in the early morning air. Nearer at hand a chimney sweep uttered his trade in deepest bass, whilst a slow-moving hurdy-gurdy provided ample competition. Then there were the fruit-sellers, and the flower vendors, all with their peculiarly individual cries, raising their voices to swell over the noise of the rumbling carriages that passed in an unending stream.

London! How different from the sights she was used to: the unending stretches of meadow dotted with patches of woodland, the gently undulating hills where the wildflowers tenaciously took root amidst the rocks, the wide arch of blue sky that seemed to form a protective enclosure for her peaceful world.

Here there was more excitement, more action. A thousand indefinable smells rose to plague her nostrils and tease her senses. Sometimes at home she would not see another person—save her father and their cook—for weeks on end, but here the people were so numerous that they jostled and rubbed shoulders with each other.

A gentle rap on her bedchamber door reminded

Halcyon that she was idling away the time instead of dressing for the day.

"Come in," she called as she drew back from the window.

She had expected her godmother's abigail, but it was not Emily who entered. Elizabeth popped her head around the door.

"I'm not disturbing you, am I?"

"No, come in. I'm afraid I'm not dressed yet." Halcyon motioned towards the open window. "I was quite rapt with wonder at the streets outside."

"Such is the comment of most visitors to this city," admitted Elizabeth. Then, laying a gentle hand on Halcyon's arm, she said, "I do hope you won't be offended, but I've brought a dress for you. It's one of mine that always has been too small for me, and I wondered if you would like to wear it for walking out today, for you seemed so despondent last night over your meager wardrobe. Not that your dress in any way disgraced you, for the color had a richness and a purity that highlighted your unusual beauty to perfection."

"How nice of you to say so," smiled Halcyon. "What a lovely gown! Are you really sure you want me to wear it? If I owned a gown like this, I don't think I could bear to see it beautify another."

"Please do wear it! And you are not offended. I'm so glad, for people can be so contrary about accepting what they consider to be favors."

"I consider it not only a favor, but a demonstration of friendship, Elizabeth," said Halcyon, "and I am deeply touched."

The gown was of embroidered white lingerie with a lace-edged petticoat. The high waist emphasized

49

the slimness of Halcyon's figure and showed her small, pointed bust to advantage. When Emily arrived to put the finishing touches to Halcyon's toilet, coiling her hair into smooth clusters of curls, Elizabeth was quite enraptured by the transformation.

"I knew that was the gown for you," she exclaimed. "And how lucky you are that Aunt Henrietta has such a skilled abigail!"

The day that followed was so filled with exciting events, one following the other in such rapid succession, that Halcyon was hard pressed to separate and identify each one.

They rode in the carriage to the draper's where, with the help of her godmother, Halcyon chose several lengths of material; they were to be delivered to Lady Hensham's house in Bath with the utmost haste so that her dressmaker might start without delay on several gowns for Halcyon.

Then followed a visit to a little dressmaker's in a side street off Charing Cross. With her usual aplomb, Lady Hensham directed that two gowns should be fashioned for Halcyon without delay.

"When will you require the gowns, m'lady?" asked the dressmaker, a small, frail woman who looked as if a hearty meal would not come amiss.

"The sooner the better," pronounced her ladyship. "In fact, if they could be ready now, I should be delighted."

The dressmaker hesitated. "I—if it please your ladyship, I have here several gowns that I keep in stock for those customers who desire immediate service. I am sure that one or two of them will need only minor adjustments to fit Miss Glaybourne." She indicated a row of gowns hanging along one side of the workroom. "Mayhap you would care to inspect them?"

"An excellent idea. Come, Halcyon, will you choose?"

It seemed almost sinful to have a choice that involved no thought of expense. Halcyon exclaimed in rapture over the wide variety and the excellence of the workmanship before finally choosing a pale blue gown with a high waist, a daringly low neck, and appliqué work on the hem; a plain white dress sashed under the waist, with short sleeves, long white gloves, and a brown embroidered shawl; and a velvet redingote that had slashed sleeves reminiscent of German Renaissance costume.

The dressmaker promised to make the necessary alterations and to send the clothes to Grosvenor Square that very afternoon.

Well pleased with their morning's achievements, Lady Hensham instructed their coachman to take a turn around the park before returning to her brother's house.

"Strictly for your enjoyment, child," she informed her goddaughter, "for I am well past the pleasure of gawking at the *ton.*"

When they arrived at the park, Halcyon saw what she meant. A never-ending stream of carriages, phaetons, and landaus rolled up and down the criss-crossing roads of the park.

The roof of their own landau was drawn back so that Halcyon could enjoy an uninterrupted view of all that was going on. Many a passing carriage was occupied by a gentleman, sometimes accompanied by a female companion. Some of the rigs had drawn to a halt at the edge of the road, where the occupants were exchanging pleasantries with friends.

"Who is that, Godmother? Just look at that splendid carriage." She referred to a rig and a gentleman who seemed to be attracting quite a lot of attention.

"My dear, that is none other than Beau Brummell —you have heard of him no doubt."

"Why yes, he sets the fashion for the *ton*, does he not?"

"Indeed, he has proved to all that fussiness and extravagance are not the essentials of good dressing, but that clean and elegant cut mean far more to the well-dressed man."

"Have you ever met him, Godmother?"

"Well, having been out of this country for well-nigh seven years, I find myself slightly out of touch, though I think it not unlikely that we shall find him—and others of even greater importance—present at various balls and soirées that we shall attend."

"Are we to stay in London, then?"

"Oh no." Lady Hensham was quite definite on that point. "I'm afraid that London begins to pall on my senses after a very few days. We shall be leaving for Bath the day after tomorrow—but make no mistake, the society you will meet in Bath is genteel and refined. Why, like as not we shall have the Prince Regent himself there for a time."

Suitably impressed, Halcyon leaned back and paid full attention to the fine gentlemen and ladies passing by.

They were superbly dressed, the ladies in their elegant muslins and cambrics, sometimes wearing one of the latest straw bonnets and carrying a tilting parasol, the gentlemen resplendent in their dark coats and light-colored breeches that fashion was now dictating should come down to their ankles instead of stopping at the knees.

"Papa still wears knee-breeches," commented Halcyon. "Is he then terribly out of date?"

"Not necessarily," her godmother assured her. "For many of the older gentlemen still wear them, particularly in the country districts."

"I do like the new style; it looks much more elegant."

She liked the Grecian style of hair for the men, too. It made most of them look devastatingly attractive, and once more she was reminded of the stranger who had kissed her in the woods as she recalled that he, too, had hair cut in this superb style.

After one or two turns up and down the road, Lady Hensham decided it was time to return to Grosvenor Square for lunch.

"Papa is taking us all to the Opera tonight," announced Elizabeth, coming into Halcyon's room after lunch.

"Oh, how exciting!" Halcyon, her eyes shining, confessed that she had never attended the opera. "And my new gown will be here, so I shall be able to dress respectably for once. Dear Elizabeth—the gown you so kindly lent me drew many admiring glances today. I do thank you most utterly."

"It was a gift, not a loan, my dear Halcyon. And are you sure it was the gown and not yourself that caused the admiration?"

Halcyon flushed. "I should like to think the latter, but I am not so vain as to suppose that I could compete in any way with the splendid ladies my godmother and I saw this morning in the park. What a sight that was! It seemed there were hundreds of carriages, and twice as many people. And we saw such an elegant beau. I pointed him out—very discreetly, I hope—to Lady Hensham, and she informed me that he was Beau Brummell himself! So resplendent, so attractive, that I could scarce keep from staring!"

"Indeed? And how was he dressed, this paragon of good taste?"

"Why, in . . . you know, Elizabeth, I can't recall." Halcyon flushed. "Why how strange! And he made such an impression on me."

Elizabeth laughed. "Never mind, I confess I was testing you, merely to prove a point."

"What is that?"

"The point that Beau Brummel himself seeks to make: that clothes should not be garish or fussy, for when they are that, they detract from the man himself and make him remembered simply for his clothes. In order to be of the very best taste, one's dress should be of superb cut, perhaps somewhat plain, and of subdued good taste. You see that Brummell is right, Halcyon, for you gained the impression of an elegant gentleman, and the details of his dress made not the slightest impression."

"Why, you're right," admitted Halcyon in surprise. "All I saw was a man of great elegance and dignity. No wonder Beau Brummell has made a name for himself in the *haut ton.*"

"All the men admire him, and half the ladies swoon over him. Can you wonder at that?"

"There must be quite a few such elegant men

about London, particularly those who frequent the Court," said Halcyon, thinking of what she had been told about Lord Rexdale's son, and wondering for the first time with real curiosity just what he was like.

"You are thinking of the marquis's son no doubt," Elizabeth guessed.

"I was," Halcyon nodded. "Do you know him, Elizabeth?"

"I have met him." Her reply was guarded.

"Then you can tell me what he is like."

"Surely your father—your godmother, too—will have already told you that. After all, you are to marry the man. They can scarcely have left you in the dark as to your prospective husband."

"But they have done just that. Oh, of course, it was partly my fault, since I was determined not to be interested in the man. I was so annoyed at being told whom I must marry, you see, that I affected total disinterest. I asked no questions and they told me nothing save that he was a very respectable gentleman, held in high esteem at Court, and much sought after by the ladies."

"Then you know as much as I can tell you."

"Really? Surely you can add something to that? His height? His build? His age? At least confirm from a young person's point of view that the details I was given are true. You know how older people look on things rather differently from us."

"I can certainly confirm that the information they gave you is correct," smiled Elizabeth. "I feel quite convinced that you will like him."

Halcyon would have pressed her further, but at that moment Jane came whirling into the room.

"I thought I should find you here," she exclaimed.

"Have you heard about our going to the Opera tonight? I do so adore the Opera!"

"What she means," explained her sister, "is that she adores avidly staring around her at the Opera. I swear she never sees anything of the show. The fashionable young ladies and their beaux—particularly the latter—are what take her eye."

Jane affected outrage. "How can you accuse me of that? You are every bit as culpable yourself of that offense—if, indeed it be an offense—even though you are already promised. And, before I forget," she added hastily, "Papa sent me to find you; he wants to speak with you in the library."

"Promised?" Halcyon gazed enquiringly at Elizabeth. "You, too? Oh, why did you not tell me? I should so love to hear about your betrothed! And here I have been so selfishly rambling on about myself and my own affairs."

"Please, don't excite yourself," Elizabeth warned her dryly. "It is scarcely a love match. I was not allowed to choose, either."

"Then we have even more in common that I thought," declared Halcyon.

"You could say that," agreed her friend, as she prepared to answer her father's summons, "although our situations are not really very similar," she added, leaving Halcyon to wonder what she meant. However, her mind was soon taken off this problem by Jane's next piece of news.

"Several parcels have arrived for you, Halcyon. Shall I have them sent up?"

"My gowns! Have they arrived so soon?"

"It appears so—also several other packages that your godmother instructed my sister and me to purchase this morning." Jane dimpled at her. "We had great pleasure in choosing for you."

Halcyon could hardly wait for the two servants to carry up the parcels. There were almost a dozen boxes of varying shapes and sizes.

"What ever can be in all these?" Halcyon cried in astonishment. She feverishly opened each in turn.

There were the three items she and her godmother had purchased that morning. These items indeed were no surprise. The other boxes soon revealed an assortment of undergarments fit to delight any princess, some frothy nightclothes—"I wouldn't dare venture out of my room in these!" exclaimed Halcyon, recalling her escapade that very morning—and several pairs of pumps and dainty slippers. There was a bag embroidered in beads, a shawl, a parasol, and a straw bonnet.

"We knew what would fit you, since one of Elizabeth's gowns fit you perfectly. Do say you like our choices."

"I-I'm speechless," uttered Halcyon truthfully. "And—and you say my godmother instructed you to buy all this?"

Jane nodded. "She said that you had need of absolutely everything, and that time was of the essence, since she had no intention of spending more than a couple of days in London."

"She's too kind. I can never hope to repay her for all this."

"Pah! You'll repay her by looking delightful," was Jane's comment. "Not only are you beautiful, but you're different from most people—in the nicest possible way, naturally."

"How do you mean, different?"

"It's hard to explain." Jane searched for words. "As if . . . as if . . . well, just fresh and natural . . . I can't describe it in any other way. I'm sure the marquis's son is going to fall madly in love with you. Just wait till—" Jane broke off suddenly and looked flustered, as though she felt she had said too much.

"Wait till what?" asked Halcyon. "And do you know him? Then, tell me, is he—"

"I won't tell you anything, dear Halcyon, because I think you should . . . well, judge him for yourself. Anyway, you're far luckier than Elizabeth, that much I will say."

There was a sudden silence in the room.

"Luckier than Elizabeth? Why?"

"Because your suitor is young and handsome and rich. Elizabeth's intended husband is only rich." Fearing that she had been far too garrulous, something of which she was often accused, Jane rushed from the room.

Her implication was clear. Elizabeth's future husband was rich and old and ugly. Poor Elizabeth! Recalling Elizabeth's earlier words about it being no love match, Halcyon realized that her new friend must be quite horrified by the prospect of her forthcoming marriage.

Halcyon felt quite dreadful about it. True, she had known Elizabeth but a few hours; after she left London with Lady Hensham, she might never meet her again. Elizabeth's circumstances should have been no concern of hers, and yet, softhearted and gentlenatured as she was, she could not rid herself of the horrifying thought, and the knowledge of Elizabeth's unhappiness hung over her like a storm cloud, as though it were her unhappiness too.

CHAPTER FIVE

The bustle and the noise of the London streets that night was quite unbelievable. As their carriage threaded its way slowly through the narrow streets where the masses of people on foot spilled over into the path of the horses and carriages, Halcyon's eyes were wide in amazement.

"You can't believe how strange all of this is to me," she exclaimed. "I have never seen so many people in all my life. What are they all doing abroad at this hour of the night?"

"Seeking amusement, trouble, or gain, Papa always says," Jane informed her. As she spoke a cry rang through the streets above the other noises: "Stop, thief!" There was a sudden movement in the thickest part of the fray. To Halcyon's surprise, a small boy, scarcely more than eight or nine years old, darted through the crowd, running like a funnel of wind through long grasses, and emerged into the road just in front of their horses. There was a shout from the coachman, the horses reared; inside the carriage they were all but thrown to the floor as their vehicle came to a shuddering halt.

Lord Cecil poked his head out the door. "What's amiss, Jason?"

Halcyon craned her neck to see if the little urchin had escaped the wheels, fervently hoping that he was safe from both carriage and crowd, for, although she knew him to be a thief, she could heartily sympathize with his desperate state.

"A wretched thief, my lord," replied the coachman, "tried to destroy himself under the wheels."

"Is he all right?" This came from Elizabeth, who looked every bit as anxious as Halcyon.

"Ay—he's off in the other direction now. Daresay he's got somebody's wallet or watch."

"Good luck to him, too," said Halcyon. "Why, he was scarce more than a babe."

"It won't do, Halcyon, to sypathize too emphatically with the rabble of the streets," reproved Lady Hensham. "True, one can feel sorrow and compassion for their wretched state, but never condone the sin of their actions."

"No, Godmother." Halcyon leaned back in her seat. Somehow the pleasure of the sight of the busy streets had quite gone, and now she felt stifled and slightly faint. She hastily applied her fan, drawing some cool air to her flushed cheeks. It was all very well to profess compassion for the poor, but how could one truly appreciate the hopelessness of their condition from the lofty perch of wealth?

Fortunately the unpleasant incident was soon forgotten, even by Halcyon, as they alighted from the coach and made their way into the Opera.

As they took their places in Sir Henry's box, the three girls gazed around them in pleasure.

"Have a care," Elizabeth warned her sister. "You know how mother hates to see you flashing amorous glances at every handsome beau."

"She won't even see," whispered Jane. "She is quite enthralled with the scene herself."

Halcyon could not take her eyes off the splendid

scene before her. The elegance of the ladies, their flashing jewelry dazzling the eyes, the fluttering of a thousand fans, all claimed her rapt attention. The attire of the gentlemen was no less inspiring; gleaming silk and brocade heavily embroidered with silver or gold thread, soft rich velvets in jewel colors, the elegance of well-tied snowy cravats, the flash of rings and jeweled snuffboxes—Halcyon was breathless to behold it all.

Suddenly her eyes were drawn to a box opposite theirs. A splendidly attired though somewhat portly gentleman was taking his place with a party of others. Halcyon knew immediately that this must be the Prince Regent, and her assumption was backed up by Jane's murmur, "My, doesn't Prinny look resplendent tonight!"

However, it wasn't Prinny but another member of his party who caused a gasp to rise in Halcyon's throat and made her heart thud with such an alarming clamor that she felt sure the people with her must hear its frantic beat.

The man now sitting on the Prince's right was none other than the charming stranger whose cravat she had secreted under her pillow! Yes, she was sure it was he! There could be no mistaking that arrogant tilt of the head, those piercing gray eyes like flashing shards of steel, that dark hair so carefully groomed to look neatly careless. He was dressed this evening in a dark-green satin coat that sported lavish gold-and-green embroidery, a gleaming white satin waistcoat with jeweled buttons, and a lingerie shirt, jabot, and cravat. He was even more devastatingly handsome than the last time she had seen him, and Halcyon, for some reason totally beyond her understanding, felt her heart turn over.

She longed to ask Elizabeth the identity of the Prince's companion, but she perceived that her godmother's eagle eye was upon her and that she had noted the direction of Halcyon's gaze.

"A handsome figure of a man, is he not?" There was a gleam in Lady Hensham's eye.

"Indeed, ma'am, a figure fit to be King," was Halcyon's demure reply. No doubt her godmother was referring to the Prince, she thought, dragging her eyes away from the dazzling object of her admiration.

Nevertheless, try as she would, her errant eyes kept returning to the handsome stranger. He was a stranger and yet not a stranger, for Halcyon had met him once, had she not? Since that meeting he had been ever in her thoughts—far too much so for her liking, for was she not promised to the son of the Marquis of Rexdale? No attraction to another, however harmless, could bode well for her. Besides, the dreams in which she had been indulging were silly, the product of an overfertile imagination. Still, it was a delight to see him again like this and to be able to feast her eyes upon him.

It was not long before he became aware of her scrutiny, and a sort of game ensued—she would gaze at him surreptitiously from under the cover of her long eyelashes when she thought his attention was elsewhere, and then would hastily glance away, cheeks on fire, when his hard, bold glance flashed in her direction.

She perceived that he regarded her with some puzzlement, and she realized that he had not recognized

62

in her the unseemly hoyden with whom he had come in contact on her father's estate, although he probably saw something familiar about her.

She smiled to herself. No wonder he did not know her. A sight further removed from the ghastly mess she must have presented on that day was hard to imagine.

She knew she looked good, and she delighted in that awareness. In fact the knowledge made her daringly coquettish, and she threw several more glances in the stranger's direction, fluttering her fan to partially conceal her face and thus give her the advantage over him.

However, when the show began, Halcyon's thoughts were only for the spectacle before her. She could not conceive that she had spent her life unaware of these great and wondrous pleasures that were to be obtained in the cities. She had never before in her life been to a theatre. She did dimly recall once having been to a fair where she had delighted in a Punch and Judy show, but it was scarcely to be put in this category.

Momentarily she forgot the man in the box opposite, and so it was that during the interval when she had just bent towards her godmother to express her unrestrained delight in the evening's entertainment, that she unwarily glanced across the theatre and unpreparedly met the full force of his impaling gaze. She gasped and felt the color go from her face. It was as though she were transfixed, mesmerized; she was completely unable to drag her eyes away from his. Their glances clashed and held, and Halcyon's heart fluttered in her breast like a trapped bird. Then a small smile played at the corners of the stranger's lips whilst his eyes took on a mocking gleam. Imperceptibly to all but Halcyon, he inclined his head in her direction; the movement caused his eyes to be cast into shadow, sending a shiver of apprehension down her spine.

Summoning a superhuman effort, she wrenched her eyes away. The telltale color suffused her cheeks, and desperately she applied her fan to chase away the heat that seemed to have invaded every corner of her body.

"Whatever is the matter?" asked Elizabeth, noting her agitation. "Are you sick?"

"No." Halcyon was mindful of her godmother's eye upon her once again. "I'm all right, Elizabeth. It is merely that the heat and the excitement of the occasion have gone to my head." The excuse appeared to be satisfactory, as all attention turned once more to the stage.

But Halcyon had learned her lesson. She steadfastly kept her eyes averted from the Prince Regent's box, and somehow survived the rest of the evening without further embarrassment.

A speedy and firm friendship developed between Halcyon and Elizabeth, so it was with the utmost pleasure that Halcyon learned that Sir Henry would be taking his own family down to Bath to spend several weeks there.

"Then we shall be able to visit together," enthused Halcyon. "I am sure that my godmother cannot have all my time planned. And as for you, you may show me all the sights, for you must surely have been to Bath before?"

"Indeed I have, many times." A flush rose to Elizabeth's cheek, and, upon being asked the origin of this, she admitted that the air, the atmosphere, and —above all—the company in Bath suited her very well.

"Elizabeth," cried Halcyon, "if I did not know better, I would swear that there was someone of particular interest to you in Bath. As it is, I am aware, as you told me, that you are already promised . . . so what, pray, is the cause of this maidenly blush?"

"It is nothing—or, at least, it is something of which I should be ashamed."

"How so? Pray confide in me, if you wish, for I can assure you that I shall hold your revelations as confidential."

"I'm sure you will. Oh, Halcyon, I sensed from the first that I had a friend in you, and I am pleased to have this first impression confirmed, for—" Her voice broke. "—I am in sore need of a friend."

"Then we shall fulfill each other's need," stated Halcyon firmly. She went to sit beside Elizabeth and placed a kind hand on her arm. "Now come, tell me, what is all this nonsense of which you speak?"

"I wish indeed it were solely nonsense. It is a problem which I am sure you yourself will fully appreciate, since the very same thing could have happened to you. You will recall how I told you that I too am promised to a man of my father's choosing?"

Halcyon nodded.

"But I consider myself far less fortunate than you, since the man I am to marry is old—older than Papa—not at all prepossessing in either face or figure, and downright ill-tempered."

"Oh, poor Elizabeth! But is there nothing you can

do? Does your father positively insist on this match? What possible gain can there be to him for you to marry this—this monster?"

"The best gain in the world."

"In truth, I know not of any gain that should outweigh a daughter's happiness and well-being."

"Except his whole family's well-being. Don't think too badly of my father, Halcyon. In truth he has almost as little choice as I do in this matter. For some time now the family finances have been in dire straits, and when Lord Medford spoke for me six months ago, offering a very generous wedding settlement, my father could scarce refuse."

"But . . . but might you not be able to—well, to attract another wealthy gentleman?" Halcyon flushed at the delicacy of the subject they were discussing. "It sounds so mercenary, doesn't it?—but surely a more presentable rich suitor can be found."

"I'm afraid it's too late for that—in more ways than one. You see," continued Elizabeth, "not only has my father already borrowed heavily from Medford, but—but—I have fallen in love with another . . ."

"Well, then," cried Halcyon, "is not that the answer?"

"My dear friend, if only it were! Unfortunately, the Earl of Winthrop is as poor as a churchmouse."

It seemed there was no answer to the problem. It upset Halcyon to think of her friend in such a predicament. And it was a situation in which she could so easily find herself, for, contrary to what Elizabeth seemed to think, she was fast becoming alarmed at the thought of her forthcoming betrothal to the Marquis of Rexdale's son. What if he was rich, handsome, and presentable? Were those the things that counted most? And how could she be sure that she would not, either before or after marrying him, fall in love with an entirely different gentleman? It was all very well to tell herself that she must guard her foolish heart, but it was fast becoming obvious to her that her heart had very much a will and a determination of its own, and showed few signs of doing the bidding of common sense or duty.

Her latest encounter with the man with the ice-gray eyes had convinced her that she was all too susceptible to the powerful attraction he exuded.

I hope I never see him again, she told herself firmly, for it would be better so. She knew the truth of this, so why, then, did the future have such a bleak aspect?

It was nightfall when they reached Bath. The journey had taken a tedious two days. Lady Hensham was querulous and Halcyon was in low spirits.

In spite of the comfort of the well-sprung landau, they had traveled in great discomfort. A deluge of rain had commenced as they were leaving London and had accompanied them all the way to their destination. It was a rain that rendered the road virtually unnavigable; the carriage had plowed its way through the mess and the mud with great difficulty, and twice they had become bogged down and had found it necessary to sit and fume whilst horses were brought from the nearest inn to pull their carriage free of the quagmire.

"I cannot understand why this road is not kept in better repair," muttered Lady Hensham angrily.

"There is surely enough passage of carriages to warrant it."

"Mayhap therein lies the problem, Godmother," ventured Halcyon, who had noticed the deep ruts made in the road by countless wheels. "The burden of constant passage is too much for the earth—why, I believe some of those ruts were at least half the depth of our wheels."

"One did hope that with the paying of a toll on these roads, conditions would improve," sniffed her ladyship. "Unfortunately it is the usual tale of being robbed blind by incompetents and thieves. If one does not get you, the other will."

"I would as lief lose my money to the former," shuddered Halcyon, as alarming images of highwaymen rose to her mind. "Are there highwaymen about these parts, Godmother?"

"Saints preserve us, child! Don't even mention such a thing! Only last summer, poor, dear Lady Charlesworth was accosted by a villain in a place very near here. Robbed of all her money and jewels, and her coachman shot dead on the spot."

It was with relief that they finally entered Bath with no greater mishaps than the fearful pictures conjured up by their vivid imaginations.

Down the London Road rumbled the coach, alongside the Avon River.

"A newly fashionable part of Bath," commented Lady Hensham, waving vaguely across the river. "The town has spread so greatly during the last few years. I'm not at all sure that I like the changes! Too much of the riff-raff here now, rubbing shoulders with genteel folk in the Assemblies and Pump Rooms." She sniffed disparagingly and Halcyon smiled a little to herself. Her godmother was as kind-hearted as they came, but not without her foibles and snobberies.

"Where is your house, Godmother?" Halcyon leaned forward in interest.

"You won't see much in the dark, child. Wait till tomorrow before you pass judgment on Bath. My house is on the Royal Crescent. See! There are the Assembly Rooms, and here we turn into the Circus . . . and so into the Crescent . . . Ah! Here we are. So nice to be back. Emily, see that our parcels are quickly unpacked. Come, Halcyon. Home at last!"

There was a pleased flush on Lady Hensham's cheeks as though she was invigorated merely by being back in familiar territory.

They were met at the door by a butler, a housekeeper, and several maids.

"Welcome home, m'lady. I trust you had a comfortable journey?"

"Worse than usual, unfortunately, Billings, but such are the penalties of traveling. Mrs. Hills, we shall partake of a late dinner in an hour. Show Miss Glaybourne to her room, and have hot water brought up immediately. Emily, I shall need you forthwith." She was in her element, nodding kindly at each in turn, issuing instructions, and obviously very pleased to be back.

The housekeeper preceded Halcyon up the wide staircase and led her to a room that overlooked the Crescent. It was a large room, beautifully furnished in grays and pastel pinks, with a large fourposter bed along the far wall.

"I hope you'll be comfortable, Miss Glaybourne," offered the housekeeper with a polite, kind smile.

"An abigail has been hired for you on your godmother's instructions, and she will be sent up to you immediately."

"Dear Lady Hensham! She thinks of everything, doesn't she?"

"If there is anything further, miss, please ring." She indicated a bell by the side of the bed.

As soon as she was alone, Halcyon explored the room in detail. It was incredible what comfort could be achieved with delicate furniture, thick rugs, and a compatible color scheme. She thought sadly of the manor house where she had been brought up, and regretted that the fine old mansion could not be brought to the state of splendor it so obviously deserved. Its rooms were drab and dingy, but nevertheless retained a vestige of their former elegance.

A gentle rap at the door preceded the entrance of a cheerful blonde girl of about Halcyon's own age. She bobbed a little curtsy.

"If it please you, miss, I'm to be your abigail."

"Come in, do!" Halcyon liked her on sight. "You do have a name, don't you?"

"Yes, miss. It's Parkes—Rebecca Parkes." Any doubts as to her efficiency were quickly dispelled as she bustled forward and removed Halcyon's travel coat. "There, miss, that's better. Now, I dare say you need a complete change of clothing—so wearying is that traveling. Was you long in coming from London?"

"Two days. I'm delighted to have you as my abigail, Rebecca. Have you been part of Lady Hensham's house for long or were you hired specially for me?"

"My sister works here, miss, and when she heard

that they was looking for an abigail for you, she mentioned my name. I haven't been—I mean I haven't had any experience, miss, but I do aim to please and I hope you'll find me satisfactory." She might be inexperienced, but she was brisk and willing, and her hands were soothing and gentle as she helped Halcyon undress.

"I'll tell you a secret," offered Halcyon with a smile. "I'm inexperienced, too. That is, I've never had an abigail before, so I expect we shall just have to learn together."

"Oooh! Isn't that nice, then! I didn't know I was going to be so lucky as to have a nice mistress like you, miss. Thought I might get one of them starchy ones—begging your pardon, miss. But, there, I'd best hold me tongue, for Emily always says that I prattle on too much."

"Emily?" enquired Halcyon rather faintly, slightly overwhelmed by this goodnatured babbling.

"Yes, she's me sister, miss—Lady Hensham's abigail."

Sisters! It hardly seemed credible. They were as different as chalk and cheese. In the few days that she had known her, Halcyon had not heard Emily utter more than a dozen words.

Noting Halcyon's surprise, Rebecca smiled.

"Hard to believe, ain't it? Well, I ain't bamming you, miss. Emily's the eldest of us, see? Left home almost ten years ago now when I was just a young thing. Always was a bit different from the rest of us . . . more genteel, like."

"Just how many of you are there?"

"Fourteen of us, miss. There, now, how's that?"

It seemed as if Rebecca's hands could move even

71

faster than her mouth. While she had been talking, she had skilfully dressed Halcyon in a fresh gown and had arranged her hair into smooth and shining ringlets.

"How do you like it, miss?"

With amazement Halcyon realized that without any effort on her part, she had been carefully and gently made ready. She felt fresh and rested; her fatigue and aches were gone.

"You're pleased with your abigail?" asked Lady Hensham after dinner.

"I am indeed, ma'am. A more cheerful disposition I never encountered."

"Hmmm." Her ladyship regarded her carefully. "She's outspoken, huh? Emily said she would be . . . was rather worried about the girl. But—since you seem to like her—"

"I do!" The truth was that Rebecca reminded Halcyon of herself, someone trying desperately to fit into a life to which she was not accustomed. No doubt she herself would make many gauche mistakes before she was finished.

"Well, child, I think you're best off to bed."

There was no arguing with Lady Hensham when she adopted that dictatorial tone. As Halcyon ascended the stairs, the front doorbell pealed and the butler went to answer the summons. Halcyon glanced back down into the hall as she turned the curve in the stairs, just in time to see a very tall figure being ushered into the library.

Her heart turned over. Surely she recognized that figure! Then she shook herself. How nonsensical to imagine that every inordinately tall gentleman was

72

the handsome stranger who had made her heart beat erratically on two other occasions. *I'm becoming obsessed with the man!* She resolutely cast the thought from her mind and continued on her way up to her room.

It was much later. Rebecca had come up and had faithfully undressed and settled her for the night, and yet, although she was tired, Halcyon could not sleep. Her whole body was tensed and strung as though waiting for something to happen.

With a heavy sigh she arose from her bed and went to stand by the window. The gaslights burned brightly in the darkness of the night. Here there was not the noise and the bustle that she had encountered in London, and Halcyon could well understand why her godmother preferred the quieter Bath. Of course, if one was interested in taking in the season, then that would be a different matter. And Lady Hensham, as she admitted herself, had had enough of that in her time. Naturally Halcyon would have been delighted to spend the season in London, but it was already half over this year, and, she was the first to acknowledge, her manners and social graces were too sadly lacking for her to appear in the very highest *ton*.

Lady Hensham had said, "You'll learn, my dear—very quickly, for you have natural poise and dignity —but for the present I feel it wiser to sojourn in Bath."

Halcyon could hear the noise of an occasional carriage as it wound its way around the Crescent, bringing home, perhaps, those who had frequented the card games or the concerts at the Assemblies. Dimly across the street Halcyon could discern the shadowy figures of sedan carriers bearing home some lady, and, just out of sight, a night watchman could be heard: *Eleven o'clock, a fine summer's night, and all's well!*

The sound of restless horses drew Halcyon's attention to the portal of her godmother's house. A carriage and four was drawn to the roadside; the coachman patiently waited at his post. Godmother's caller must be still with her. What could be delaying him? she wondered, for she knew full well that he would not have left his equipage at the front had he not intended to leave almost directly.

As she stood and watched from her window, she heard muted voices, the sound of a door closing, and then footsteps ringing out on the stones.

A tall figure came into view. Oh, it was . . . no, surely it couldn't be—and yet! Halcyon leaned forward and pressed herself against the glass to examine the gentleman to greater advantage. He looked up, right to her very window, and she saw the brilliant flash of his eyes and knew of a certain that it was he. Too late to draw back; he must have seen her. She was certain it was so when she caught a gleam of white teeth in the moonlight. Oh! Her cheeks blazed. She stepped back and hid behind the curtains till the noise of receding wheels told her that he was gone.

CHAPTER SIX

The next days passed in a whirl for Halcyon. There was so much to do, so many new activities to enjoy. Lady Hensham took Halcyon in hand and instructed her in various points of social behavior she felt she should be familiar with.

For her part, Halcyon was an apt and willing pupil, although privately she believed much of this necessary etiquette to be rather a sham and ridiculous. However, she did not voice these opinions to her godmother, which was just as well in the circumstances.

Since their arrival in Bath there had been a steady stream of parcels and packages arriving from Lodnon. The little dressmaker off Charing Cross had done her work well, and Halcyon now had clothes that would not disgrace the finest duchess.

Halcyon wondered many times about the gentleman caller her godmother had received on the evening of her return to Bath, but although her curiosity was strong, she dared not show too much interest in the matter. The wonder of it was that her godmother herself had mentioned nothing of the matter. Halcyon recalled now that Lady Hensham must also have seen this gentleman in the company of the Prince Regent at the Opera, and yet she had not acquainted Halcyon with his identity.

Halcyon shook herself in annoyance. And what

was so strange about that? She was reading some-thing mysterious into what had been no more than an innocent oversight. Indeed, why should her god-mother acquaint her with the gentleman's identity? Surely it was nothing to her. She was not supposed to be interested in every casual caller, and it would be deemed a gross indelicacy if she—already prom-ised to the future Marquis of Rexdale—were to show inordinate interest in another gentleman.

So, much as she would have liked to have broached the subject, she held her tongue. Control over her tongue she might have, but control over her curiosity she certainly did not, and her thoughts ran riot.

Why am I so interested in him? she asked herself many times. Why does a picture of him impose itself behind my eyes when I lie in bed at night? Why do my thoughts turn to him countless times during the day?

She was well aware that her thoughts should be directed rather towards the as yet unknown suitor. It would have been more natural for her to have been consumed by a desire to know him, instead of which all she felt was a rather tepid inquisitiveness. Time enough to think of him when their proposed betroth-al became a reality, she told herself.

Her godmother was teaching her how to embroi-der, a skill of which hitherto Halcyon had been sadly ignorant. Much to her surprise, she discovered a natural talent for this task, and Lady Hensham ex-pressed great satisfaction in her aptitude.

"Who would have thought you to have such a gift, Halcyon?"

"I fancy, ma'am, that you had quite taken me for

a bluestocking," her goddaughter remarked with some amusement.

Her ladyship nodded her gray curls.

"I confess to being agreeably surprised on more than one occasion, my dear. This is but one of several ladylike pursuits to which you have taken like a duck to water."

"A far stretch from the ragamuffin you first encountered?"

"Happily so!"

They were seated in the drawing room a week or so after their arrival in Bath. They had spent many hours thus sitting, each with her embroidery on her lap, sometimes talking, sometimes placing their chairs over near the long windows from where they had a superb view of the activities of the Crescent.

Lady Hensham put down her embroidery.

"Halcyon, my dear, I think we are sufficiently rested and well enough settled here now that we may start to receive callers. My friends in Bath know well enough how I dislike to receive until I am recovered from the rigors of travel, and that is why we have so far seen no one. However, today I shall put the word around that we are receiving."

"Shall we have many callers?"

"You can bank on it. I shall send a note around to my dear friend Lady Cranshaw, and thereafter you shall see how the acquaintances arrive."

"You must have many friends in Bath, ma'am."

"A goodly number—but all the more now, I fancy, since I am rumored to have staying with me a delightfully winsome female guest."

"You flatter me, ma'am. But how will they know that, pray?"

"My dear, you underestimate the channels of gossip in this town. From the very first day, their conversation will have included you."

"How could they know?" persisted Halcyon. "We scarcely issued a bulletin on the subject."

"The servants, my dear. They talk, you know—not indiscreetly, mind you, for I would not tolerate that, but already they will have imparted details of your age, your appearance, and your delicate manners . . ."

"You make it sound, my lady, as if I were in the marriage market. Since I am promised to the marquis's son, there will scarcely be a line of eager suitors outside the door."

"Nay, do not sound so bitter, Halcyon, my love," reproved Lady Hensham. "Have I not made it clear to you that I have brought you to Bath not merely to learn the social graces and to gain experience of meeting and mixing with people, but also to enjoy some girlish fun? A commodity in which your life has been sadly lacking, I fear."

"But ma'am . . ."

"You look surprised!" Lady Hensham chuckled at the expression on her goddaughter's face. "Didn't think I harbored such sentiments, did you? Well, you were wrong, child. I know how a little harmless enjoyment plays an important part in life. I've had my moments, too, you know!" Her pale blue eyes sparkled as scenes from the past flashed across her memory. "Ah, yes, indeed I have!"

Halcyon fancied that she must have misunderstood her godmother's meaning. Surely Lady Hensham was not suggesting that Halcyon should enjoy all the pastimes and pursuits of a young lady who was seeking a suitor?

"Have you forgotten, ma'am, that the marquis—"

"The marquis's son is of the very same opinion as mine," stated her ladyship firmly. "We have agreed that you are to have a time of respite before your betrothal, a time when you may feel free to enjoy whatever pursuits you please—within the bounds of propriety, naturally."

"Naturally," echoed Halcyon, quite nonplussed by this latest development. "But surely the marquis's son will expect—"

"I am sure he expects nothing save that, when the time comes, you will willingly accept his suit without bitterness and without rancor for not having been allowed to choose your husband."

"How noble of him," murmured Halcyon with mixed feelings. Privately she was thinking that either he was a man blessed with a kindness and an understanding far beyond his years, or he was perhaps no more in favor of their prospective betrothal than she was. "And when may I hope to meet this paragon of virtue, ma'am?" In spite of herself, her curiosity was piqued; what kind of a man would allow his future wife such a free rein?

"Oh, I daresay you'll meet him in good time, my dear," was Lady Hensham's vague reply.

Not to be fobbed off with this, Halcyon persisted in her questions. "But surely I shall meet him in the near future? We are not to be kept apart until our betrothal, are we?"

"Be patient, miss!" Lady Hensham sounded vexed. "There is no secret about his identity, and of course you will meet him in good time. But the man has given you an opportunity of which you should be grateful, and you can hardly expect him to come rushing to your side simply to comply with a whim on your part. No hint of your betrothal has been cast abroad. You are free as the air you breathe—to use the young man's phrase—and I hope you are cognizant of the very considerable inconvenience to your intended."

"I am, I am. Only, it does seem a little out of the ordinary."

"Of course. When you meet him, you will find that the marquis's son is not an ordinary man."

"Pray forgive me, Godmother, for laboring the subject, but I would know one more thing. Does the marquis's son frequent Bath? Am I like to meet him in this city?"

"He has a house in Bath. You may meet him at one of the Assemblies. As far as you and he are concerned, you will be nothing more than new acquaintances—do you understand?"

"Very well, Godmother . . . though it does sound rather strange." Halcyon did not know what to think of the matter, but since she had been handed the opportunity to see something of life without the encumbrances of a fiancé, she felt it would be unwise to offer any hindrances to the scheme.

Lady Hensham had been right about the callers. That very afternoon they had their first visitors.

Upon receipt of her ladyship's note, Lady Cranshaw had come to call with all speed and eagerness. Accompanying her were her son and daughter, William and Clementine. The former was a rather intent young man, impeccably dressed and possessed of perfect manners, whilst his vivacious sister was a year or two younger. Lady Cranshaw herself was a small, bustling woman who had every appearance of having her whole life under strictly regulated control.

"My dear Henrietta," she cried on entering. "How delightful to have you back amongst us once again. And no doubt your sojourn this time will be rather more extended than usual, will it not? Dare we hope that you and your charming goddaughter will be wintering here in Bath?"

"Indeed, such is my intent," Lady Hensham assured her. "I have promised Halcyon that she shall taste all the joys of Bath."

"In that undertaking, I am sure that William would be of utmost willing assistance."

"Certainly." William inclined himself graciously, "I can conceive of no greater pleasure and privilege than that of escorting Miss Glaybourne."

"Well——" began Lady Hensham, a dubious frown on her face.

"Nay, Henrietta, do not deny us this pleasure. It will be of the utmost propriety, since Clementine will naturally accompany them."

"In that case, I am sure that Halcyon will be agreeable to his escort on occasion, my dear Clarissa. But, pray, tell me all the news, for I am sadly out of touch. I did hear that the Earl of Stevens has finally spoken for Melissa Maybury's hand."

"That was scarce any surprise. He has been mooning after her for many a long month." Lady Cranshaw sniffed. "Though what he sees in the insipid miss, I shall never know."

Lady Hensham smiled to herself. Such sour grapes

were only to be expected of her ladyship, for had she not hoped to strike a match between the Earl and her own daughter, Clementine?

"Come, now, mother," remonstrated that young lady, "you well know that Melissa is a sweet thing, and it is quite naughty of you to call her insipid merely because she is not as garrulous as the rest of us."

"Well, sweet she may be, but she certainly lacks sparkle. For the life of me I cannot imagine why the Earl did not prefer someone of a more vivacious, lively manner. Heaven knows—"

"Come now, mother, we have been into all that before," put in Willaim, no doubt seeking to spare his sister's discomfiture. "And, personally, I can think of many men in Bath of equal eligibility."

"Yourself for one, of course," simpered Lady Cranshaw, "for it will be a lucky young thing who finds herself favored by you."

"I take it you are referring to my financial eligibility, ma'am, since only this morning you took me to task over my behavior," replied her son somewhat stiffly.

"Fie! To think that you would throw that in my face! You know my advice is only for your own sake, William, though I must say that much of it falls on stony ground."

"Come, Clarissa, every young man needs to sow a few wild oats."

Lady Hensham's support of her friend's son was tantamount to treachery, and Lady Cranshaw threw her a withering glance.

"I'm afraid we cannot all hold your modern ideas, Henrietta."

82

To this Lady Hensham merely smiled, then turned the conversation to a less abrasive subject.

"Don't pay any heed," whispered Clementine to Halcyon. "They always carry on so. Why, I do believe they enjoy sparring constantly. But, say, my dear Miss Glaybourne, do say that you will accompany us to the Pump Room in the morning, for there you will meet the *ton* and make the acquaintance of many new friends, I am sure."

"I shall be delighted, if Godmother has no objection."

"Splendid," said Lady Cranshaw across the room. "And perhaps you would both care to call on us tomorrow evening, for we are having a *thé* in your honor, to celebrate your return among us."

CHAPTER SEVEN

The Cranshaw carriage called early for Halcyon the next morning. She had dressed with particular care, as this was to be her first public appearance in Bath and she desired to make a good impression.

She now had a most extensive wardrobe, since the materials which her godmother had bought in London had arrived at the house, and Lady Hensham had lost no time in hiring a dressmaker to prepare several striking outfits for her goddaughter.

Halcyon wore a delightful creation in white muslin, elaborately sewn with pink and blue roses; there was a ruffled frill around the hem, beneath which poked her tiny feet encased in dainty blue pumps. Her gleaming red ringlets were pinned with a spray of flowers to which was added a curling white feather. A blue parasol completed the picture.

"Pray do not forget your reticule," said Lady Hensham, handing it to her as she prepared to sally forth on William's arm.

"How adorable you look," cried Clementine as she made her appearance at the door. "But then you have natural good looks—even mother commented on that fact yesterday when we arrived home."

"I am indeed flattered to be so admired," murmured Halcyon, feeling that some expression of pleasure was warranted, but nonetheless flustered.

"Come, sit beside me," encouraged Clementine. "I

shall point out the sights to you as we go along. Is this not your first visit to Bath?"

Halcyon laughed. "In truth, it is almost my first visit anywhere. I have been brought up in the country, and I must confess to be totally lacking in knowledge of the towns."

"Then you will find Bath all the more delightful, Miss Glaybourne," William assured her, "and this city will be all the more fair for your presence."

In the face of this excessive praise from one whom she had thought to be somewhat retiring and shy, Halcyon blushed and showed signs of confusion, whereupon Clementine laughed delightedly.

"I see that you were taken in by my brother's serious air. It is a pose he affects, for he says it pays handsomely in the eyes of strict mamas who would fiercely guard their offspring from undesirably boisterous characters."

"Really?" murmured Halcyon, gazing at William with new eyes. She had noticed immediately the change in him from the previous day.

"I was in the company of my dear Mama, and therefore on my best behavior."

"Mother can be so quarrelsome," sighed his sister. "And you should hear her sharp tongue. I expect you gathered by the tone of the conversation yesterday that she had designs for me to marry the Earl of Stevens?"

"Such was my impression," admitted Halcyon.

Clementine laughed. "Do not appear so embarrassed for me in that area, dear Halcyon, for I assure you that *I* had no such hopes or desires. Indeed, I have yet to meet the man who completely blinds my senses, though if Mama had her way I should be married off to the first rich and passably good-looking man who came along."

Halcyon assumed that the dear Lady Cranshaw was something of a martinet, and Clementine confirmed this opinion.

"Poor father, now, is not at all of the same disposition, thank goodness. No, he is amiable and good-natured—very easy-going. He would do anything for a peaceful life, whereas mother's main ambition seems to be to deprive him of it. I declare that she never gives him one moment's respite, the result being that he frequently escapes to the gaming rooms, where he fritters away each evening. Mama is constantly scolding him that if he does not manage to dissipate his fortune before his demise, William will no doubt follow in his footsteps and complete the job."

Clementine showed no sign of ceasing her constant chatter, but her brother was not to be done out of his share of Halcyon's attention.

"How you do prattle on, Clemmie! Do have a mind for Miss Glaybourne's pleasure. She no doubt wishes to enjoy the sights of Bath without your voice for accompaniment."

Clementine had the grace to look ashamed.

"I'm sorry. Papa says my tongue too often runs away with me. Look, Halcyon, we are passing through the Circus, and in a moment we shall proceed down Gay Street to Queen's Square, which is where our house is situated. See, there it is on the far right—but you will see more of that tonight."

The streets became narrower, and Halcyon discerned that they were entering the older part of the city.

"Some vestiges of the old walls remain," William pointed out.

"See, here we are coming to the Orange Grove—and the Abbey; is it not a splendid building?"

Now the carriage was coming to a halt before an impressive façade.

"The Grand Pump Room," announced William, jumping down from the carriage. "Cummings, pray return for us at ten."

As she descended from the carriage, Halcyon was quite taken with the beauty of the building. The portal was fully two stories high, supported on four Corinthian columns that gave a majestic air to the whole. On either side of this there were smaller entrances of lesser impressiveness. A railing ran in front of the long front windows, blocking them from the road and the crowd of people who either walked or rode nearby. There were carriages picking up and depositing visitors to the Pump Room; there were chaises and Bath chairs bearing invalids.

Inside, the impression of grandeur was scarcely diminished. Here Corinthian pillars duplicated those outside; the full-length windows let in the bright sunlight, and a niche in a wall at the far end of the room contained a statue of Beau Nash, the man known as the "King of Bath" at the beginning of the previous century.

Halcyon soon became acquainted with the purpose of the Pump Room. It seemed that one could partake of the waters, if one so desired, but Clementine had nothing favorable to say of this pastime.

"Utterly horrible, my dear," she declared with a delicate shudder. "Ask William if you do not believe me. The water must indeed be very salubrious, to judge by its taste—for are not all things that are declared to be good for us slightly repugnant?"

Halcyon felt she could hardly disagree with this argument.

"Forget about the waters," urged William. "Let us parade up and down, and we shall soon see someone with whom we are acquainted. Why, I do declare! There's old Henley himself. Pray excuse me, ladies, if I desert you momentarily." He hurried off to greet his friend.

"You must not mind William," declared Clementine, "or think him ill-mannered. He will be assured of your indulgence, I know, when I tell you that he is totally enamored of Lord Henley's sister."

"Then I shall not mind his desertion," declared Halcyon.

The two of them continued their walk. Halcyon thought she had never rubbed shoulders with so many strangers, and she was not at all certain that she found this activity as enjoyable as Clementine appeared to find it.

"Are you sure that you see no one of your acquaintance?" she whispered urgently to Clementine after they had taken a turn or two up and down the room. She was feeling quite put out of countenance by the stares of so many strangers.

"Let us go and look at the arrivals," suggested her friend. "The book will inform us of any new visitors of note."

Halcyon was all too soon disillusioned with that occupation, too. It became obvious that her companion was scarcely interested in the book so much as in the stares of two bold-faced gentlemen standing nearby.

Clementine flashed them a coy glance, and Halcyon was horrified to note that they showed every intention of approaching.

"Oh, Clementine, how could you encourage them so?" she remonstrated.

"Fiddlesticks!" said she, laughing. "The Pump Room can be a very dull place if one does not do something to liven it up. Besides, they are quite harmless. In fact, I quite fancy the one on the left—does he not have a devil in his eye?" She dimpled at the gentleman in question.

"Clementine, I do declare that I shall turn around and leave you if you persist in this encouragement! I may be gauche and countrified, but even I can tell that those two are not of the top drawer." She viewed with distaste the garish dress of the pair. "Pray, let us collect William and depart."

"Not so fast. Do not upset yourself. I promise to be good." Clementine laid a placatory hand on Halcyon's arm. "What say you we take a turn down the other side of the Pump Room?"

Having no means of returning home without the Cranshaws' carriage, Halcyon was forced to comply. She was acutely aware of a fundamental difference in attitude between herself and Miss Cranshaw, and she was surprised at this. Aware that Clementine came from the best of families, she was amazed by her coquettish demeanor. Was this accepted behavior? Oh, she hoped not. I could never learn to act so boldly, she told herself. I must be more of a prude than I suspected!

This thought amused her greatly, and it was thus that she was smiling when she looked up and noticed a gentleman who was standing conversing with some friends. Her mysterious beau! For this was how she had begun to think of him.

The color swept into her face as she regarded him. His clothes, his manner, the deference shown him by his companions and several of those who passed by, all proclaimed him to be of the highest *ton,* and Halcyon found herself greatly admiring his elegant stance. He was dressed in a chocolate-brown coat and smooth fawn trousers with a matching waistcoat that showed corded brown embroidery. His snowy white shirt, trimmed with lace at the cuffs, matched his intricately tied cravat.

Suddenly he turned and looked her directly in the eye, as though he had been aware all along of her approach. Was it impertinent to stare so boldly? She suspected it a strong possibility but nevertheless found herself just as mesmerized as before by his gaze. It was Clementine's voice by her side that brought her to her senses.

"Well, I do declare, Miss Glaybourne! And you presume to lecture *me* on encouragement! How is it then that you dare to regard the eligible Lord Anthony Dray so boldly?" Do I take it that you know this gentleman?"

"No-o-o . . ." admitted Halcyon. "Though I believe he is acquainted with my godmother." She lowered her eyes and turned resolutely away from the gentleman. But she thrilled to think that at last she had found out his identity.

"How then did you find the Pump Room?" Lady Hensham asked her at breakfast.

"Tolerably interesting, ma'am," was Halcyon's reply.

"How so? Only tolerably?" Her godmother was surprised. "Do I detect a moue of discontent?"

"No, Godmother, pray do not misconstrue my remarks. The drive through the streets of Bath was decidedly pleasant. How impressive I find the buildings! The Abbey has an aspect which left me totally breathless and overwhelmed. As you will naturally appreciate, since you are aware of my classical education, the immense buildings, with their Corinthian or Ionic pillars, represent in my mind the dignity and drama of a bygone age. I can think of no other architectural style that pleases me more."

Lady Hensham regarded her searchingly for several moments. It seemed to her that her goddaughter's remarks were somewhat evasive.

"Hmmm. Yes, well . . . you like the buildings. But it was about the Pump Room I asked you, and my enquiry was not directed to its architecture."

Halcyon decided that total honesty should exist between herself and her godmother. Where was the sense in subterfuge?

"To tell you the truth, ma'am, I found the crowd unappealing. Mayhap it is my too-long sojourn in the country that has made me uncomfortable in crowds, but I find it distinctly onerous to dawdle around a hall full of people, jostling with some, rubbing shoulders with others. And so many strangers staring at me quite put me out of countenance. I fear you have under your wing, ma'am, a gauche country bumpkin."

"Don't fret yourself on that score, Halcyon. I confess to exactly the same sentiments myself. Ah, Bath is not the same as it was in my youth, my dear. Then the society in the baths and the Pump Room was of the highest *ton*. How I deplore the changes today! Unfortunately, one must move with the times and accept the changes brought about by progress. And what did you think of Lord Cranshaw and his sister?"

"A most lively pair, ma'am. Clementine proved every bit as talkative as my abigail, Rebecca."

"Hmmm. Too fast a tongue is not becoming in a lady."

"No, ma'am."

"I fear poor Clarissa will have her hands full with that pair. But enough of the Cranshaws. Let us speak of more enjoyable things. This afternoon I propose to go down to Milsom Street. There are still various purchases I wish to make on both your behalf and my own. I have a fancy for a new silk reticule, and you must have a mantelet for this evening, I think."

"Why, I should like that, ma'am! I saw a handsome one this very morning, worn by a lady in the company of Lord Anthony Dray."

"Lord Dray? What do you know of this gentleman? I was not aware that you had been introduced. Pray, tell me the events of this morning, for I feel you have left something missing."

"No, no, indeed," murmured Halcyon in confusion. "I was not introduced to the gentleman—Clementine merely mentioned his identity to me." She would, she perceived, have to be more careful of her tongue in future.

"I see. Well, no doubt introductions will come soon, for I myself am well acquainted with the dear man, and therefore you may expect him to be a fairly frequent visitor to the house."

Lady Hensham's prophecy proved quite correct, for that very afternoon as they returned from their outing to Milsom Street, a carriage drew up before the house as they were entering the front door, and, to Halcyon's surprise and considerable delight, Lord Anthony Dray alighted.

"My dear Dray!" exclaimed Lady Hensham. "We were discussing you only this morning."

Lord Dray bent over her outstretched hand. "Indeed? Then I hope your comments were favorable."

"Oh, I do assure you that they were of the highest order. I am delighted to see you, Dray, for it is high time that you made the acquaintance of my goddaughter, Lucius Glaybourne's daughter. Halcyon, this is Earl Dray."

"A pleasure I have long been awaiting." His lordship smiled, bowing low. "Your humble servant, Miss Glaybourne." Was there a sparkle in his eye? Halcyon could detect no amazement, no change in his countenance as she was introduced. She had expected some surprise as her identity was revealed and he recollected their first meeting in the grounds of the manor, but not a muscle moved in that handsomely chiseled face.

Could it be that he had already recognized her as the hoyden in the woods? Her cheeks flamed—oh, she hoped not!

Seated in the small salon, Halcyon was able to study him as he exchanged pleasantries with her godmother.

Suddenly he turned to address her. "I trust you are enjoying your sojourn in Bath, Miss Glaybourne?"

"I am tolerably well amused, sir," she replied, feeling that the conversation sadly lacked in warmth and genuine interest. Why, she felt as if his lordship were already a friend and acquaintance of long standing, so often had he been in her thoughts. She had expected—nay counted—on being greeted with a smile, instead of which she found herself confronted by a cold and distant stranger.

Her lack of pleasure communicated itself to the earl, and his dark eyebrows winged up quizzically. "Only tolerably well? Do I take it then that our fair city lacks charm in your eyes?"

"No, indeed," she hastened to correct herself. "I did not mean to sound disparaging about the city—which, so far as I have seen, is of delightful aspect."

"Then it must be the company that is not to your liking."

Worse still! What a gauche mess she was making of this conversation!

"I—I find that more than adequate, my lord." She lowered her eyes. He was being deliberately obtuse, she felt sure, amusing himself at her expense, and the thought angered her.

She was puzzled and out of countenance. He had made no reference to their previous meeting, as though it were some offense to have offered his assistance when she had hurt her leg. No doubt he was merely being circumspect, but it was not pleasing to her, this verbal fencing, this thrusting and parrying as though they were fighting a duel instead of renewing a small acquaintance.

She shook her head in vexation and then looked the earl straight in the eye. Maybe it was not correct social behavior to come right out and speak one's mind, but it was her way, and she could act no differently.

"I fear you are annoyed with me, my lord."

"How so? What gave you that impression?"

Lady Hensham hastened to intervene; the conversation was taking a turn which she felt incomprehensible. "Lord Dray is only bamming you, my dear Halcyon. Pray do not tease the child so, Dray. She is unaccustomed to these little quips of yours."

"I am afraid I am unaccustomed to everything to do with the ways of the *haut ton*!" exclaimed Halcyon. Then, turning to her godmother, she admitted, "I feel as if I am part of a play and that I have been left on center stage with no book of lines. The other characters come and go, and I fumble in agony for the right lines!"

"Now what brought this on?" Lady Hensham looked from Lord Dray to Halcyon, sensing something uneasy between them.

"I must confess that I have not been entirely frank with you, Godmother. I—Lord Dray and myself have already met."

"Already met!" Lady Hensham's startled gaze met that of his lordship. "How can it be that you told me nothing of this, Dray?"

"I was not aware," said Dray slowly, "that Miss Glaybourne would like to admit of the meeting."

"Explain, please," was the terse rejoinder.

"What Lord Dray means," explained Halcyon with dignity, "is that we scarcely met in the best of circumstances, and were not then formally introduced, as I believe social etiquette requires. Nevertheless, I was grateful to Lord Dray on that occasion, for I had suffered a small mishap and he was able to be of considerable assistance to me. It was that very day you called on my father, ma'am. In the woods

I had had the misfortune to cut myself; thanks to Lord Dray's skilfull administrations, I suffered no lasting harm." She stood up. "And now, if you will permit, I will leave you. No doubt Lord Dray will be able to enlighten you further, should you so desire."

With a haughty nod she swept from the room, but once she was alone in her own room, her frustration and anger overcame her and she threw herself on the bed and let enraged tears flow.

"Am I interruptin' you, miss?" Rebecca's soft voice intruded on her thoughts.

"No." She sat up on the bed and wiped away her tears. "Do come in Rebecca. Oh, I am in such a flurry of anger! How hard it is to know what to do and how to act. I fear I have made an utter cake of myself."

"Yes, miss," said Rebecca, not understanding in the slightest. "Is something wrong?"

"How my head pounds! As though the anger and frustration were hammering to get out."

"Here, let me brush your hair for you. I'll be gentle as I can, and that will relax your nerves, miss."

Under Rebecca's soothing ministrations, Halcyon's tangled emotions calmed.

"Your touch is magical. How lucky I am to have you! Oh, Rebecca, I find myself at such odds with myself! My emotions seem at such variance. Only this morning I was decrying Clementine Cranshaw's lack of decorum and excess of free speech, and yet this afternoon I myself took exception to the finer points of social etiquette. At one moment I wish to be refined and aloof, and the next moment I would throw caution and dignity to the winds."

Rebecca's comment was direct as usual. "You sure you're not in love, miss?"

"Whatever makes you say that?" Halcyon stared at her in surprise.

"Begging your pardon, miss, if I spoke out of turn —only the maids in the parlor was discussing it just the other day. Said being in love made you feel all contrary like."

"They are likely right, but I cannot claim that to be the root of my problem. Why, I have met very few gentlemen, and know none of them well enough to be in love."

"Lawks, miss, yer don't have to know 'em to love 'em! Leastways, that's what my friend Sally says. And she should know!" Rebecca's speech had been slowly improving, but in her sincerity she dropped back into her former ways. "Sally says—"

"She's probably right," interposed Halcyon hastily, for she rather suspected that the admirable Sally's knowledge arose from an experience that went far beyond the bounds of propriety.

All the same, after she had dismissed Rebecca and lay once more on her bed, dry-eyed this time, she pondered on Sally's dictum. Could one fall in love as easily and as simply as that? She had always supposed this emotion to grow only after long and intimate acquaintance. Had she been wrong?

Needless to say, her thoughts flew to Lord Anthony Dray. It was undeniable that she felt drawn to him, and for what reason she could not analyze. The attraction he exuded every time she met him had her positively quaking in her shoes, as though expecting a shaft to dart from those magnificent eyes of his and pierce her trembling body. But love? Nay, that was ridiculous. She was mesmerized by the man because of the romantic circumstances in which she had first met him, when he had come to her aid like a knight on a charger, an answer to a maiden's prayer . . .

Yes, she was attracted to him—but it was a flimsy emotion, the product rather of her childish daydreams rather than of any momentous reality. Why, if the truth be known, she did not even like the man. For how could one like someone who treated one with the cold contempt and aloof arrogance that Lord Dray had shown today?

No, she did not like him. She had, however, liked the gentleman who had bathed and bandaged her leg. He had changed in character since then. She had thought him to be a rather charming, unconceited gentleman on that occasion. What then had caused this reversal she now felt? Was it her identity? She recalled how his face had closed and the warmth had gone out of his voice when she had told him she was Lucius Glaybourne's daughter. Did he now stand on distant ceremony with her because of her relationship to Lady Hensham? Or was the change in his manner caused merely by the fact that he was disposed to be friendly and familiar with the serving wench he had at first supposed her to be, but he could on no account extend the same liberties towards the lady he now knew her to be?

Whatever the reason, he was different. Halcyon fretted sorely over the change.

Downstairs in the salon, Lord Dray swung violently away from the window.

"I'm not sure we've done the right thing, ma'am."

99

"Why ever not? I thought it was working surprisingly well."

"Hmmm . . ." He regarded her searchingly. "Mayhap too well."

"What makes you say that? Did we not hope for success of our little ruse?"

"Yes, of course. Though I must confess that I did not expect to see such early signs of it."

"It was that first meeting that did it. What a romantic adventure! Why did you tell me nothing of this, Dray?"

"Truth to tell, it was rather a pleasant shock for me. And, upon examination, I found it a delightful memory—all the more delightful for being a secret."

"'Pon my word! I believe you find the girl attractive!"

"Can you wonder? Her looks are unusual and exceptional."

"But not just her looks, Dray. Come, now, admit more than that shallow appreciation!"

"She does intrigue me," admitted the earl slowly. "So different from the rest, you know."

"She herself calls that difference 'gauche.' "

"Never! Have you observed the way she moves? The way she holds her head, and that expression, that . . ."

"My, my! You *have* been scrutinizing her!" Lady Hensham appeared to find the matter highly amusing, although Lord Dray's agitation was nothing to be laughed at.

After several moments of serious contemplation, he raised his head. "We made a bargain, you and I, ma'am—a bargain that I fear I can no longer keep."

"Why, how so? Fie, my lord, you must keep your word or everything will be ruined."

"Are you sure the whole thing will not back-face on us?" The earl's face proclaimed his grave doubts. "Have you considered what will happen if the lady in question falls in love with me to the point of refusing to marry the future Marquis of Rexdale? That would prove a pretty pickle indeed! I'm not sure that this plan of ours is not a flagrant tampering with her affections."

"Nay, nay, Dray, do not meet trouble before it rears its head. Halcyon will enjoy a romantic interlude before the reality of her marriage to Rexdale's son. And if she falls in love with you, I am still convinced that she will do her duty and turn her matrimonial hopes towards Rexdale."

"Even so, I have no wish to inflict a humiliating experience."

"Have no fear, my dearest Dray. I know the workings of a woman's heart. All will end well." Lady Hensham nodded her head complacently, and after a moment of intent perusal of her serene countenance, Lord Dray agreed with her.

"Very well. We will continue as planned. At least this way I can be sure that no other man will trifle with her innocent and guileless affections."

Halcyon came downstairs feeling ashamed of her undignified outburst and intending to apologize to her godmother. She was surprised and somewhat disconcerted to discover Lord Dray alone in the salon.

"I beg your pardon, my lord, I was looking for my godmother."

"She has momentarily gone to her room. But wait!" he called as Halcyon turned and would have disappeared too. "I would like a word with you."

"Very well," said Halcyon, coming back to stand before him. She surveyed him coolly from under her gold-tipped lashes. "I have some moments to spare."

"Good Lord!" He swung away from her and went over to the window, where he stood contemplating the comings and goings in the busy street.

Halcyon stood patiently, awaiting his words.

He seemed to be fighting a battle with himself as he stood there. Undecided emotions flitted across his face. She thought he looked sad and a trifle bitter as he gazed unseeingly at the passing carriages. Finally he appeared to make up his mind, and he came back across the room to her side.

She noted with wonder that the arrogance and coldness had gone from his eyes.

"Sit down, Miss Glaybourne," he urged, "for I find it hard to apologize whilst you are standing."

"A-apologize?"

"Yes. I do owe you an apology, you know."

"What ever for?"

"Well," he said, seating himself beside her on the wide sofa, "first of all for the undignified kiss I snatched from you on the occasion of our first meeting. I cannot say that I am sorry, for it was, in fact, a most exquisitely enjoyable experience. But it was not the act of a gentleman. Pray accept my profuse apologies on that score, ma'am."

"You thought I was a serving girl." A smile played around Halcyon's lips. "You were shocked when you discovered my identity."

"Yes." He regarded her searchingly. Surely she did not suspect!

"I wasn't much of a lady, was I?" she said sadly. "I wonder that you could bear to touch me in my dirty, disheveled state! And yet you did. You cleaned my cuts and treated me with courtesy and with gentleness—the true mark of a gentleman. You thought I was a lowly peasant, and yet you had nothing but kindness in your heart . . . About the kiss we will say no more, since your other actions robbed it of any blame."

"How kind of you to say so. I take it, then, that I am restored to your favor?"

"Were you ever out of it?" She smiled across at him.

"I fancy so. An hour ago you withered me with one glance."

Halcyon laughed. "Indeed I did no such thing. You are, I suspect, a man not easily withered, my lord."

"Mayhap you are right." His gaze was direct and penetrating. "Then we can begin again, Miss Glaybourne. And as proof of our goodwill towards each other, may I presume that you will favor me with a dance at the Late Summer Ball? You will be attending, will you not?"

"I—I scarcely know. You will have to ask my godmother that."

"Ask your godmother what?" asked Lady Hensham, entering the room at that very minute. "What are you two planning?"

"Lord Dray is merely asking if I will be present at the Late Summer Ball, Godmother."

"Naturally so, my dear Dray. You know I would

103

not miss it for the world—although I fear the crush will be intolerable. Ah, I remember when . . . but you will scarcely want to hear my reminiscences, my dears."

When Lord Dray had taken his leave, Lady Hensham expressed her delight. "A charming man, Halcyon, and a most eligible one, too."

"You're forgetting, are you not, that his eligibility can have little meaning for me, Godmother. I am not searching for a husband, merely a—"

"Rubbish, my dear. Eligibility is very important, whether it be in a suitor, an escort, or a friend. I am delighted that Lord Dray so obviously finds you attractive."

Halcyon threw up her hands in despair. It seemed that Lady Hensham was even more of a romantic than she herself was.

CHAPTER EIGHT

The *thé* at the Cranshaw's was a glittering affair. Lady Cranshaw prided herself on her entertaining, and nothing but the best would suffice for this, her welcome-back *thé* for her dearest friend.

The house in Queen's Square was lavishly decorated. The polished wood furniture shone to an extent that rivaled the crystal of the sparkling chandeliers; flowers were arranged in profusion, their color reflected on the tabletops and in the countless mirrors on the walls, and their perfume mingling with the amber musk scent favored by the ladies.

Lady Hensham and her goddaughter were ushered in with great dignity and respect. Cries of delight and expressions of pleasure greeted their arrival. There were at least a hundred guests, and Halcyon could only be amazed that the house would hold so many.

Not being aware of exactly what constituted a *thé*, Halcyon looked around her eagerly. All the guests had assembled shortly after eight o'clock and were now grouped at small tables, which were laid as for breakfast—with a napkin at each place, tea and coffee, and an assortment of rolls, wafers, bread and butter, and a load of buttered muffins. To partake of such a repast so soon after a six-o'clock dinner seemed to Halcyon the surest road to indigestion.

After downing large quantities of the food so lavishly provided, the guests mingled and gossiped, and some retired to an adjoining room to play cards.

Halcyon was introduced to so many people that her head reeled, and she was sure that she would never recognize any of them again.

In her estimation, the new rage for the *thé* party was highly overblown—it was no more than a fancy name for a boring gossip session. When she confided as much to her godmother later in the evening after their return to the house in the Royal Crescent, the latter was inclined to agree with her in part.

"Yes, it is an occasion for the older people, I must confess. You young ones prefer the hustle and bustle of activity in Milsom Street, where you can watch the coming and going of Bath notables; or the dancing in the Assembly Rooms—or even walking on the hills that surround Bath, so I am told. Never mind. I dare say you shall have all the excitement you so crave when you dance at the Assemblies with Dray."

If it seemed to Halcyon that her godmother was inordinately eager to press on her the attentions of Lord Dray, she tried to push the thought to the back of her mind. Indeed, the whole matter of her sojourn at Bath seemed out of the ordinary. Having been informed of her duty to marry the marquis's son, she expected to have been whisked away to his care and attention, instead of which she found herself indulged in several weeks of reprieve and, stranger still, allowed—nay, encouraged—to enjoy the company of others. The Marquis of Rexdale's son must be a strange man to allow his future wife such liberties. Halcyon could not help but feel a little piqued by this casual attitude. Did it not show on his part a lack of affection that amounted to a disinclination to take the path of duty dictated by the promise made by his father to her mother at the time of her death?

Well, far be it for her to refuse to take advantage of the circumstances in which she found herself. If the marquis's son was disinclined to come forward and claim her now, it was scarcely anyone's fault but his own if Halcyon enjoyed her freedom to the fullest. Her conscience thus salved, Halcyon looked forward with mounting pleasure to the Assembly Ball.

Surveying herself in the long mirror in her room, she was well pleased with her appearance. Nothing could be further removed from the tattered hoyden image she had presented to the earl on the occasion of their first meeting. Her dress was of sheer silver tulle over a satin underdress; the waist was gathered high under her bust and fell in full folds to within a few inches of the ground, allowing a glimpse of her satin-shod feet. Her hair had been dressed to form curls on the top of her head, a glistening mass of shining coils that caught the light and reflected startling highlights. Yes, she really would do, she decided, with a small trace of vanity—surely forgivable in one who seldom showed that trait.

Her cheeks were flushed and her eyes sparkled in anticipation of the joys of the evening ahead, adding to the totally enchanting picture she made.

The carriage was brought around to the front and she stepped inside behind her godmother.

The night was soft and warm. A bright full moon rode high above in the wispy clouds, imbuing them with a silvery ethereal incandescence. The roofs of the Royal Crescent were etched dark against the glowing sky, and the streetlamps dotted the landscape like miniature moons. The carriage swayed and rumbled slowly over the cobbles, in no apparent hurry to arrive at their destination. There were many other equipages heading in the same direction, as well as several groups of people walking and a scattering of chairmen scuttling out of the way of the carriages as they bore ladies to the ball in their sedan chairs. The moonlight cast their elongated shadows onto the cobbles, giving the whole scene a strangely unreal appearance as if the darting figures and equipages were cardboard cutouts against a backdrop of cardboard houses.

Lady Hensham had been right about the crush in the Assembly Rooms. Such a milling of people!

"I enjoy the music and the conviviality, my dear," said her ladyship now, "but the crowds quite overcome me. Come, let us make for the other side of the hall, for I think I see Lady Cranshaw and Clementine."

"How nice to see you, my dear," called Lady Cranshaw. "I was just this minute remarking to Clemmie that I hoped we should see you here, though it is quite dreadfully crowded, isn't it? Oh, I do declare! There is the Earl of Brampton. I had not heard of his return to Bath . . . So delightful to have you amongst us again, my lord," she murmured as a tall, fair-haired man approached the party. "Have you been long back from your travels?"

"Lady Cranshaw, a pleasure as usual. And Miss Clementine, looking more beautiful than ever." The earl bowed over their proferred hands and then turned to Lady Hensham. "I see that you, too, are returned from far-off places, ma'am. And is this your

108

goddaughter whose beauty has set the city of Bath agog?"

"Lucius Glaybourne's daughter, Halcyon," affirmed Lady Hensham as the earl took Halcyon's hand.

"I met your father once, Miss Glaybourne—at least so I am told—but I must confess that I was too young at the time to appreciate the pleasure. But to return to your question, Lady Cranshaw, I returned to Bath last week, and mighty pleased I was to be home, too."

"Come, now," simpered her ladyship, "I hear that Paris is full of most enjoyable pursuits for a gentleman such as yourself."

"True, but Bath boasts the most beautiful ladies on earth, don't you know." He grinned amiably at the ladies and was rewarded by their blushing smiles.

Actually Halcyon thought his compliments slightly overdone, but he appeared to be a pleasant young man. Her roving eyes noted the arrival of Lord Dray. He was superbly outfitted in a blue satin coat that did little to conceal the breadth of his shoulders, and white inexpressibles that clung to his well-shaped legs. His black shoes had silver buckles that gleamed in the light. Halcyon's eyes moved swiftly over him, noting his impeccable appearance, the skillfully tied cravat that Beau Brummell himself could not have knotted more adroitly, the ruffled shirt with a touch of embroidery that matched his coat.

If Halcyon's appraisal was a trifle bold, his was none the less exacting. The piercing intentness of his gaze met hers across the room and brought the color to her cheeks. Then he came forward and greeted each of the ladies in turn.

"I see you kept your promise to be here," he whispered to her, drawing her unobtrusively away from the others.

"Did you doubt that I would?" asked Halcyon in surprise.

"Ah! You ladies have capricious minds! And some of you like to tease."

Halcyon tossed her curls. "Not I. I would scarce play such childish games, my lord," she told him emphatically, bringing the laughter to his eyes as he noted her serious countenance.

"What a refreshing change you are, Miss Glaybourne! So lacking in guile."

They were standing by the open windows, and Halcyon raised her face to gaze up at the inky blue heavens.

"What a nice night it is . . . almost too perfect to remain inside, even for the pleasure of dancing. It was on nights such as this that I used to walk in the woods with the silence of the stars overhead and the tiny scuffling noises of nature around me in the trees and undergrowth."

"You mean you used to go alone in the darkness of night?" asked Dray, watching the expressions of pleasure flit across her face as she remembered. "Were you never afraid?"

"Afraid?" Halcyon turned to him in puzzlement. "Afraid of what? The darkness?"

"Many ladies are afraid of the dark," insisted his lordship. "But, no, I was thinking more of the wild animals that so often frighten those of your tender sex . . . or of lurking strangers who might wish to do you harm."

Halcyon smiled. "Those 'wild animals' that you

110

mention were more often more afraid of my passage than I of theirs—and as for strangers, we seldom saw any in the vicinity."

"Nevertheless, had I been your father, I think I should have been concerned for your safety."

"You mean you think he failed in his paternal duties?" she asked sharply, always ready to contradict any implied criticism of her darling parent.

"No, no, nothing like that," Lord Dray hastened to assure her. "I was not condemning his laxity. In fact, I rather admire him for allowing you a freedom that obviously taught you serenity and self-assurance. Although I confess I should have been unable to tolerate with a quiet mind the knowledge that you were roving alone around the countryside at all hours of the day and night."

"You find me self-assured?" asked Halcyon curiously.

"Yes." He glanced quickly at her. "You sound as if that surprises you."

"It does. I have never thought of myself as self-assured—rather the contrary, in fact. I am not one of your elegantly sophisticated ladies of the Court, you know," she reminded him. "I have had a very different upbringing."

"A very permissive one?" he hazarded.

"In a way, yes . . . But also, you see, it was very restrictive." She sensed that he waited for her to explain this last statement. "It is true that I was perfectly free to roam as I pleased, but my life was sadly lacking in companionship—save that of my dear papa, naturally—and I scarcely ever saw or communicated with another human being in the course of a whole year. Christmas always brought in a few friends and well-wishers, but apart from that I have led a singularly solitary life, one which I would scarcely have thought would give me the self-assurance that you mention. Indeed, I am nervous when confronted by strangers and quite put out of countenance when they stare at me—as they did when Clementine and I visited the Pump Room two days ago."

"Yes, I confess I noted your confusion," he laughed, recalling the incident. "But I do assure you, Miss Glaybourne, that my appraisal was only of the highest admiration. But that is not what I meant by assurance. I meant rather that quiet sense of knowing oneself and being contented with what one is—a very poor attempt at an explanation, I'm afraid."

"No, I do understand what you mean, and, after all, I have had plenty of time to examine my own company. On the other hand, you will no doubt find me gauche in the execution of the social graces and niceties observed by the *ton*. I trust you will not be ashamed of my performance, my lord."

He was astounded by her words and momentarily bereft of a suitable reply. "Performance? What a strange word." Then, catching a glint of humor in her eye, he continued, "Ah! I see you are bamming me, Miss Glaybourne. Yes, indeed, as your word implies, conforming with the silly little rules of society does seem rather like putting on a little act, a false front to face the world. I recognized by your reaction to my nonsensical subterfuge when your godmother introduced us a couple of days ago that you felt nothing but contempt for both verbal simpering and sparring."

"Oh, I hope . . . I was rude, wasn't I? I'm truly

sorry!" She turned a penitent face towards him. "You see, that's what I meant by gauche."

Lord Dray laughed. "No apologies needed. In fact, I liked what you did. I saw at once that you were a young lady of genuine feeling and unaffected character. No, let me assure you that if this is gauche, then I shall not be ashamed to be in your gauche presence this evening."

The evening was quite without parallel. Halcyon had never enjoyed herself so much. Lord Dray led her out to the first dance of the evening and thereafter danced with her two more times. As her circle of acquaintances was speedily widening, she did not lack for partners. She discovered that the Earl of Brampton, inspite of his propensity to dish out compliments to all and sundry at the slightest provocation, was in reality a pleasant gentleman, and by the way his eyes constantly strayed to Clemmie Cranshaw, Halcyon deduced that his interest in that young lady was sufficient to gladden the heart of Lady Clarissa.

"Are you intending to stay in Bath through the winter, Miss Glaybourne?" he asked Halcyon as he whirled her into a cotillion. "And how is it that we have not seen you grace our city before now?"

"I believe my godmother intends to spend the winter in Bath, my lord." She could scarcely speak for her own presence—who knew whether Rexdale's son would whisk her away before then? "This is my first visit to Bath; my father lives some distance to the north, which no doubt accounts for my being out of the public eye," she added dryly. She knew that such a statement was a lie by omission, since even had her father's estate been on the outskirts of Bath, their sadly depleted financial state would not have allowed her the freedom of Bath and its society.

"Ah, then you are from the country." Halcyon had heard this statement expressed often enough with a wealth of scorn underlying it, but the way the earl said it made it almost a compliment. "The towns are all very well, are they not? But one does so sadly miss the country. Here in Bath some of us have the best of both worlds, though. You must come out to my country house some day. I shall remember to speak to Lady Hensham before the evening is out."

He was as good as his word. Later that evening Halcyon approached her godmother, who was deep in earnest conversation with the earl.

"My dear Halcyon," called Lady Hensham, "do come over here, child, and hear the splendid proposal of Lord Peter. He has had the marvelous idea of a houseparty to be held at Brampton Court. Three whole days to enjoy the fresh country air; it does get so stifling in town in August!"

"It is indeed a generous suggestion, Lord Peter," declared Lady Cranshaw, determined to applaud his invitation as loudly as her friend. She had not been unaware of the earl's attention to her daughter.

"I shall have the invitations prepared and sent out forthwith," declared the earl. "Needless to say, yours will be the very first to be dispatched."

"A most satisfactory evening, all in all," was Lady Hensham's verdict when they returned to the Royal Crescent. "How did you enjoy your first ball, Halcyon?"

"Very much, ma'am. It was all the more exciting

for me, since it was far removed from the sort of life I have experienced hitherto."

It had indeed been a splendid evening. Halcyon's mind went over and over all that had happened; she recalled the bright lights, the glowing ballroom, the lavish and colorful gowns of the ladies, the glittering jewels of duchesses and countesses. The handsome men! The breathless gaiety of the dancing!

And Lord Anthony Dray . . . What a fine figure he had cut!

CHAPTER NINE

As Halcyon walked down Milsom Street, there was a flush on her cheeks and a pleased smile of contentment on her lips. She had just purchased the most delightful bonnet with flowers cascading down one side of the crown and floating green ribbons on the brim. Now all she had to do was buy the embroidery silks that had been the original objective of her outing, and then she could make her way home.

It was a delightful day. As usual the streets of Bath were crowded; a flurry of people hemmed the roads, whilst the passage of countless equipages excited her interest and curiosity. Halcyon decided that she would walk back to the Crescent; it was not so very far after all, and she enjoyed the excercise.

"Why Halcyon, what a pleasant surprise!" Clementine was beckoning to her from the doorway of the pastry shop. "Just when I was bemoaning the lack of a companion to share a sinful indulgence with me. What do you say? Will you join me for a pastry or two?"

"Why not?" laughed Halcyon, entering to shop with her friend.

"You have made a purchase?" asked Clementine, her quick eyes noting the hatbox Halcyon carried. "Is that something to wear at Lord Peter's houseparty? Did you get your invitation?" she continued without waiting for a reply. "Lord Peter brought ours around the very next day after the ball! Oh, Halcyon! I am so happy! Did you notice the attention his lordship paid to me? My dear, I am positively in a spin! Which cake will you have? You should try one of those little puffy things with the fruit and cream inside. Mmmmm! I can't resist them. Happiness does so increase my appetite—though I shall have to be careful now that I have at last done something of which my mother approves. What do you think of the earl? Is he not divine?"

Halcyon perceived with amusement that this was going to be a very one-sided conversation. "He is indeed a very presentable gentleman," she confirmed. "Clementine, has he—"

"Spoken for me? Not yet!" Clemmie took a bite of her pastry. "But he will, I am convinced of the matter."

Halcyon could only be glad for Clementine; indeed she seemed a different girl since love had struck her. How wonderful to feel secure and warm in a man's love, thought Halcyon. I wonder if I shall feel that way about Rexdale.

Arriving back at the Crescent, she almost collided with a figure leaving her godmother's house.

"Miss Glaybourne!" exclaimed Dray. "I have just now been visiting your godmother and expressed my sorrow at having missed you."

Halcyon was sorry, too. "I—I had some errands, and as the weather was so fine I was persuaded to walk back instead of taking the carriage." She was stammering and her face was flushed, she knew. Why, oh why did she behave like a gauche country miss with the very person she desired so desperately to impress?

"The exercise has brought a quite becoming flush to your cheeks," smiled Dray, deliberately mistaking the reason for her rosy countenance. "But I regret that I cannot tarry. Your godmother assures me that you will both be accepting Lord Peter Brampton's invitation to his country home this weekend. No doubt I shall see you there." He saluted her, waited till she had passed through the door of Lady Hensham's abode, and went on his way.

"Lord Dray was here but a moment ago," her godmother informed her. "He professed himself disappointed to have missed you."

"Yes, I met him at the door." Halcyon affected indifference. "I understand we are to accept Lord Peter's invitation. Will there be many guests, do you suppose, ma'am?"

"Some twenty or thirty, I believe. Did you match all the embroidery threads you need?"

"Mmmm. I also purchased an adorable bonnet, godmother. And I met Clementine Cranshaw in Milsom Street. We sampled some pastries together, and Clemmie was utterly full of Lord Peter. It seems that—"

"Yes, I know." Lady Hensham threw up her hands and smiled. "Lady Cranshaw was here earlier and could talk of nothing else. It seems that at last in her eyes poor Clementine has been able to do something right. I do wish Clarissa would not ride the girl so. Leave her to find her own suitor in her own way, was what I told her years ago, but she wouldn't listen. Paraded poor Clemmie around like a piece of goods at a slave market! Huh! Too eager by far to marry the girl off. Still, at last the girl has attracted an eligible male—with no prodding from mama, either. Clarissa was almost speechless with surprise and delight. She quite expects the earl to speak for Clemmie in the very near future. I do hope she's not being premature, though."

"Oh, no! Clementine gave me the very same impression, and I rather think that she . . . well, that she knew more than she was divulging."

"You think so? Then mayhap we can expect an announcement this weekend," suggested her ladyship. "Talking of which, Halcyon, we must decide which gowns to take. You have not yet worn the pearly pink peau de soie."

"It's too long, Godmother."

"Then it must be altered. Go and try it on, child, and we shall see what is to be done."

As Halcyon became used to finding her way around Bath, she went out more and more without the carriage. The house on Royal Crescent was not far from the main shopping area, and it was far simpler to walk there than to descend from the carriage in a busy street and be obliged to give explicit instructions regarding the time and place when she would be ready to return.

But Halcyon became too accustomed to the streets and therefore careless.

The very day before the Earl of Brampton's houseparty, Halcyon was in Bath searching for just the right shade of green ribbon to tie around her hair. She had started her search in Milsom Street, but had somehow managed to wander into the side streets. As the roads became narrower and the buildings pressed in on her on every side, she was startled to realize that her quest had brought her to an area with which she was not familiar.

The people around her were not only strangers, but were of a type that she knew instinctively would wish her more harm than good. A couple of ill-clad beggars stared at her boldly, their eyes shifting from her face down her slight form to the reticule that dangled on her arm. Halcyon clutched it more firmly to her and quickened her pace.

Oh, if only she had not been so foolish as to leave the main streets! She picked up her skirts and ran down the whole length of one street, turned a corner, and saw yet another narrow alley ahead of her. Oh dear! How would she extricate herself from this?

She could hear running footsteps in her wake and she knew she was being followed. Ahead of her she saw a small ragged boy, disconsolately wandering down the street, his bare feet dragging on the dusty cobbles. He glanced up at her with interest. Then she saw by the widening of his eyes that something was happening behind her. She whirled around to feel a heavy blow to her side, and her purse was wrested from her arm. Then she was thrust to one side as a dirty beggar made off with her reticule.

Everything happened so fast she was powerless to do anything about it. But the small beggar boy was quick to react. He stuck out a grimy foot as the thief rushed past him, tripping him and sending him sprawling into the gutter. Then he grabbed the reticule and held on tight. The thief let out a few oaths, sprang quickly to his feet, and advanced on the boy.

" 'Ere! 'And it over, yer varmint! It's mine, see!"

"No it ain't! It's hers!"

"What's it to you, then? 'And it over, I says!"

He pounced on the boy, sending him reeling into the wall and cracking his head against the stones with such force that a stream of blood spurted out onto the cobbles. But still the boy held on to his treasure.

At this point Halcyon was not sure whether the boy meant to return the reticule to her or keep it for himself. Either way, she could not let the little fellow be hurt by the big bully.

"Let go of him!" she cried shrilly. With more courage and strength than she had thought herself capable of, she threw herself into the fray, kicking and pounding the man with her small fists. It appeared as if he would fight back; then, suddenly, with a fierce, crude exclamation, he glanced up the street and took to his heels.

Turning around, Halcyon perceived that two gentlemen had rounded the corner of the street and were speedily coming to her aid.

She turned back to the urchin.

"Are you—" She found that she was addressing the empty air, for the rascal had taken to his heels in the wake of the other ruffian. Her reticule lay at her feet.

"Well, by the saints!" exclaimed a familiar voice. "Miss Glaybourne, what on earth is happening here?" Lord Dray retrieved her reticule and placed it in her hands.

Now that the worst danger was over, Halcyon felt absurdly weak in the head. She clutched Lord Dray's arm. "How glad I am to see you, my lord!"

"I should think you are!" She looked up in surprise at his harsh, clipped tones, and instead of sympathy in his eyes saw only anger blazing there. "What the devil were you doing in this part of town, Halcyon? Did not your godmother warn you against the dangers of walking unescorted abroad? By gad! So this is what comes of your lenient upbringing!" He smote the palm of one hand with the fist of his other and Halcyon thought he would have liked to lay his hands on her for this apparent misdemeanor. "I swear, if you were my daughter, I should whip you for this piece of nonsense!"

Halcyon drew herself up to her full height.

"Then it's fortunate that you are not my father, my lord, and as such have no jurisdiction over me." She was angry at the way he had spoken to her and angry that he was somehow disappointed in her. She dusted her skirts with an impatient hand. "And now, if you will be so good as to point out to me the nearest way to town, I shall relieve you of my irksome presence."

"Nay, not so fast!" He grasped her arm to prevent her escape and turned quickly to the other gentleman at his side. "I shall settle this matter, George, and return forthwith. Now, Miss Glaybourne, I shall escort you home and instruct your godmother that she would be well advised to pay greater heed to your excursions."

He led her unprotesting through the alleys. Not that she was in any way grateful to him or calm in the face of his high-handedness, but she suddenly found that she was quite glad of his assistance since she had an intolerable stitch in her side where the ruffian's blow had hit her. It was for this reason that she leaned against Lord Dray's arm rather more heavily than the circumstances dictated. Glancing quickly down at her pinched, white face, he realized that she was hurt.

Halcyon swayed and stumbled as the street swirled around her blurred vision and the cobbles heaved and rose like the waves of an angry sea. With an exclamation of concern, Lord Dray caught her before she fell.

When her eyes opened, Halcyon was lying on a divan in a strange room. She heard an indistinct murmur of voices behind her and struggled to sit up and take note of her surroundings.

Lord Dray hurried forward. "Easy! Rest quietly, Miss Glaybourne; everything is all right."

Still not totally in command of her senses, Halcyon heard her own voice mumbling somewhat foolishly, "You called me Halcyon before . . ."

"And so it shall be again, if you wish," smiled the earl. "But for the present, lie still."

"Where am I? What—oh!" At once she remembered.

"You are at my town house. I have dispatched a message and carriage to your godmother, and presently she will be here to ascertain for herself that nothing worse has befallen you than a few bruises and a rather nasty shock. Do you feel better now?"

"Y-yes; I think so."

"Good." He sat down at the foot of the divan. "Then perhaps you feel like telling me exactly what happened."

"Did you not see it all?"

"Most of it . . . I can guess the rest. Upon my word,

Halcyon!" She noted that the anger—or was it merely frustrated exasperation?—was back in his voice. "You see where the foolishness of your actions led you?"

"It was not foolishness," she protested. "I was looking for some green ribbon. I lost my way and before I knew it I was in the narrow alleys and these two thieves came upon me . . ."

"The old man and the boy?"

"No, no!" She shook her head. "The boy wasn't one of them. There were two men. One of them disappeared and the other lunged at me and stole my reticule." She shuddered at the mere memory of it.

"And the boy?"

Halcyon leaned back and closed her eyes. She could see the urchin with vivid clarity in her mind's eye. She heard again the frightening thud of his head against the wall and saw the blood gush forth.

"He came to help me." She was almost sure of that, although she had thought for a moment that he too had been tempted to steal her reticule. "He—he was hurt. I hope he was all right."

"Bound to be. These beggars are tough. Now let this be a lesson to you. I want you to promise that you will not venture down the side streets again, is that understood?"

"Yes, it's understood," Halcyon replied evasively, careful to commit herself to no promise, for already the idea was forming in her head that she would have to make inquiries to see that the lad was not too badly hurt. Beggar or not, he had a right to some humane consideration. Besides, something in his face, a kind of empty despair, had moved her to the deepest compassion. She knew that she just had to pursue the matter further.

However, she was careful not to tell his lordship anything of this. The less he knew, the better.

CHAPTER TEN

Brampton Court lay just outside Bath, nestled in the rolling green hills. The surrounding countryside was lush and green; a trout stream wound its way through part of his estate, and deer grazed in the parkland behind the house.

The house, constructed of honey-colored Bath stone, glinted warmly in the setting sun as Lady Hensham's carriage rode up the winding elm-bordered drive. Halcyon alighted with her godmother and they mounted the flight of wide stone steps, passed through the huge portico graced with elegant Corinthian pillars, and were greeted by Lord Peter at the entrance to a huge baronial hall.

Halcyon stared around her in amazement. It was all so grand, so spectacularly beautiful! A circular oak staircase wound upwards from the far end of the hall, divided at one level and branched into twin curves that circled the perimeter of the hall with a gallery.

Laughter emanated from the various open doorways around the hall, and Halcyon surmised that many of the guests had already arrived.

They were conducted by a maid up the stairs and round the gallery to where large double doors led through to a small private suite consisting of two bedrooms and a sitting room.

They scarcely had time to look around them

before Emily entered, divested them of the manteaux, and efficiently smoothed into place any stray curls that had become disarranged by the journey.

She had already begun her task of unpacking their valises as they made their way downstairs to join the rest of the guests.

"What a splendid idea of Lord Peter's to have his guests arrive in the evening," commented Lady Hensham. "It makes the preliminaries of the stay far less onerous and gives one the opportunity to acclimatize oneself gradually. My dear Halcyon, you will be expected to hold such events when you are Lady Rexdale, so mark well the smooth running of this household. The earl's mother is well-known for her entertaining, which is entirely *comme il faut.*"

Four large rooms on the ground floor were being used by the congregating guests.

In the music room the piano was being played by Lord Peter's sister Emma, a dark pretty girl with a lively countenance, whose attention was being sought by no less than three gentlemen standing around her.

Halcyon smiled to herself. She had heard that men swarmed around the excellent Lady Emma, but that as yet she had shown no undue haste to end their misery by choosing one of her suitors.

Double doors at one end of this room led out to a salon. Halcyon could see Clementine and her mother conversing with Lord Peter, and in the background, near the open french windows, Lord Dray stood beside a tall dark man whose acquaintance Halcyon had not made.

As she moved into the room, Lord Dray came forward and took her arm. "Miss Glaybourne, I should like to introduce you to a great friend of mine, the Earl of Winthrop. Charles, Miss Glaybourne is Lady Hensham's goddaughter."

"Delighted to meet you, Miss Glaybourne."

Halcyon stared at him frankly, noting the thin, sensitive face, the soft brown eyes, and the humorous tilt to his mouth, and decided that she liked what she saw. So this was the gentleman on whom Elizabeth had bestowed her affection.

"It is a pleasure to make your acquaintance, my lord, particularly since I have heard my friend Elizabeth Cecil talk of you so often." It wasn't quite the truth, of course, but she couldn't resist seeing his reaction to Elizabeth's name.

The earl's eye kindled warmly.

"Indeed? You are a friend of Elizabeth's? Then I must confess that I am doubly delighted. And since we have discovered a topic of mutual interest, may I be so bold, Miss Glaybourne, as to suggest a stroll in the garden?" He gestured towards the french windows. "The night is balmy and pleasant, and no doubt we shall be able to find a seat under the trees in spite of the popularity of the gardens this evening."

As Halcyon nodded her acquiescence, Lord Winthrop took her arm and turned to his friend, Lord Dray. "You will excuse us momentarily, Dray?"

Scarcely pleased with the turn of events, Dray could do little about them. He nodded stiffly to his friend.

Lord Winthrop merely wanted to talk about Elizabeth, Halcyon suspected, but did Lord Dray know that? His face was dark and pensive as he watched them disappear into the darkening garden where the shadows stretched in purplish fingers across the lawns.

"My dear Miss Glaybourne, pray do not think me too forward," smiled the earl. "I fear I have annoyed Dray—but I see by your countenance that you understand very well why I have shamelessly lured you out here."

Halcyon nodded. "You wish for news of Elizabeth?" she asked composedly.

"Indeed, yes! Have you seen her? Is she well? Ah, I see by your face that she did take you into her confidence."

"Merely very briefly, I am afraid. I must confess that I have not seen her more recently than two weeks ago in London. She was well, but scarcely happy. You must know that her family intends coming to Bath in a few days, but to Elizabeth's chagrin Lord Medford will be accompanying them."

"Egad!" expostulated Lord Winthrop, smiting his palm against his forehead. "You are sure of this?"

"Yes," Halcyon nodded. "I received a letter from Elizabeth but two days ago."

"Then this ruins all our plans," the earl cried in anguish.

"Nay, it is surely not as bad as that," Halcyon remonstrated. She liked the earl, but she was uncertain as to how much she should encourage him and Elizabeth to see each other and to feed the fire of their affection. She sympathized wholeheartedly with Elizabeth, but she could see nothing but acute unhappiness resulting from a denied love. Since Elizabeth had to marry Medford, would it not be better to get it quickly over with and to blind herself to what might have been between herself and Lord

Winthrop? She would scarcely make a good wife to Lord Medford with the sharp blade of anguish thrusting in her breast. Better to turn away the earl right now . . . better not to know the sharp pleasures of love . . . better to . . . better to be dead!

This last thought came to Halcyon with piercing clarity as though it were a cry from her own heart. If Elizabeth had to marry a man she disliked and despised, surely it should not be denied her to indulge a warm and true affection for Lord Winthrop prior to her marriage. Would that not give her something to hold dear in her memory through all the bitter years ahead? But hold on, she told herself. Aren't you becoming too emotionally involved in this? What business is it of yours? It is for Elizabeth and Winthrop to make that decision—and for you as a friend to do what you can to help them.

The earl was speaking again.

"You are very silent, Miss Glaybourne."

"I was thinking of Elizabeth . . . and you . . . and how to appease both conscience and love."

He regarded her seriously.

"Yes," said the earl. "That is the problem, is it not? Well, they say the course of true love never does run smooth. May I ask a favor of you, Miss Glaybourne? A very large favor?"

"What is it?"

"That you—er—conspire to bring Elizabeth to meet me as soon as she arrives in Bath. I was accustomed to communicating with her through her maid, but this person has been dismissed, I understand. Whether anyone suspected that she was carrying notes between the two of us I do not know, but it seems likely. This necessitates my finding other means of communicating. What do you say? Will you do it?" The earl was hard to resist. He did seem so sincere, and Halcyon well knew Elizabeth's feelings in this matter.

Nevertheless, she hesitated. How deeply did she wish to become involved? It was all very well to condone the romantic couple's actions—but to play an active part, a prominent role in the deceit, was surely another matter.

"I—I cannot say, my lord." She bit her lip in perplexity and her large green eyes glowed in the light spilling out through the windows of the salon. "I—I think I should wait till I speak with Elizabeth on the matter."

"But you will speak with her?" persisted the earl.

"I will indeed," she promised.

Their return to the salon was noted by a pair of cold gray eys, and Halcyon's heart sank with a lurch of dismay. How hard it was to please everyone! Now Lord Dray was angered by her prolonged absence in the garden with Elizabeth's young man. Not, of course, that he realized that Lord Winthrop was enamored of Elizabeth—Halcyon felt certain of that, else why would he be regarding her now, his icy eyes disdainfully flickering over her and then dismissing her with contempt?

No doubt Lord Dray thought she had been dallying with his friend in the bushes. The color rose to Halcyon's cheeks as she realized the injustice of this. It irked her that she could not clear herself without divulging Elizabeth's secret. Besides, what business was it of his whom she chose to walk in the garden with—or even what she did there? He didn't own her; he had no claim on her; he was not her keeper! Only the Marquis of Rexdale's son could remotely claim that privilege, and he had shown scant interest in that direction.

She boldly returned Lord Dray's stare and tossed her head haughtily, an action which brought a smoldering response to his eyes. She felt quite certain he would have come to her side had not Clementine claimed her attention at that point.

"I was looking for you earlier on, Halcyon, but you had disappeared. Where on earth have you been?" she asked, and straightaway continued without waiting for an answer. "Never mind. At last I have found you, and I shall just burst, my dear, if I do not tell someone my news!" Her curls bobbed excitedly as she positively shivered with excitement. "Come into the alcove where we can have some privacy."

She led the way back into the music room, where the long curtained windows provided a natural recess into which were set padded seats.

"Here we can be alone now that Emma has finished delighting her lovesick gentlemen," Clementine mocked. "Oh, dear! That was rather a nasty thing to say, was it not?—particularly as I am so happy myself and Emma will soon be my sister-in-law. But one does so envy those gorgeous creatures who have such a seemingly limitless choice of suitors. But, my dear Halcyon, as I was saying, she is to be my sister-in-law, and you know what that means? Yes! The earl called on Papa last night. He spent simply ages with him in the library, but when they reappeared they were both positively beaming from ear to ear. Yes, before Christmas I shall be the

Countess of Brampton! Just think of it, my dear! Do say you're happy for me!"

"Of course I am! Particularly as the match is a suitable and happy one. Not everyone is so fortunate."

"Oh, how right you are! I mean, think of poor William."

"What of poor William?" asked Halcyon. It was news to her that he had any problem save that of an overanxious mama.

Clementine was only too happy to impart the information. "You know how he is smitten with Lord Henley's sister, don't you? Quite a useless waste of affection and energies, my dear, for that lady's parents are quite determined to make a countess out of her by arranging an alliance with the Earl of Winthrop."

"Oh!" gasped Halcyon. "Is this true?"

"Why, yes." Clementine regarded her friend in some surprise. "Whatever is the matter, Halcyon? You are looking positively deflated! Don't tell me you feel so strongly about William's forlorn love?"

"I—no—it's nothing," muttered Halcyon, belatedly trying to cover up her reaction. "Nothing at all."

"Come now, you dark horse!" Clemmie was not to be fobbed off quite so easily. "That news hit you a deadly blow—now don't deny it. I wonder why? Oh no! I have it! *You* are in love with the Earl of Winthrop! Oh, Halcyon!" Clemmie stared at her in dismay. "I had heard a rumor—who hasn't?—that the earl was secretly in love with a penniless sweetheart. Sorry, my dear, but you must admit that your father has nothing. Oh, dear! What a confusion, I do declare!"

"No, you've got it all wrong!" Halcyon found her tongue at last. "It's not like that at all. Why—"

"Say no more." Clemmie held up her hand. "If you feel you cannot confide in me, it is quite all right."

Halcyon would have protested further, but at that very moment they were interrupted by the approach of Lord Dray, whose unfortunate opening remark only convinced Clementine further of her discovery.

"There you are, Miss Glaybourne. I trust you had an enjoyable stroll in the garden with the Earl of Winthrop?"

Clemmie triumphantly rounded on Halcyon.

"There you are! I knew it!" Her eyes flashed in excitement at this new piece of gossip she would have to impart. "Don't worry, Halcyon. Your secret is safe with me," was her maddening parting shot as she swept past the earl and returned to the salon, leaving Halcyon to meet with dismayed consternation his lordship's condemnatory scrutiny.

Why should I care what he thinks of me? What does his opinion of me, good or bad, matter? Halcyon asked herself later that night when she was at last alone in her room. Lord Dray had been quite insufferably frigid for the rest of the evening—an attitude which he had no right to assume. Just because he is a friend of my godmother's, he seems to think that he has some sort of hold over me. Well, he is wrong! I thought he was a courteous and kind gentleman, but I perceive that I was wrong. His barbed comments, his sly innuendos this evening were quite uncalled for; I shall be careful not to encourage him in any manner or form in future.

But why, oh why did his good opinion so obviously mean something to her, try as she would to convince herself otherwise? I scarcely know that man. No doubt I am merely mindful of the two times he has come to my aid. Yes, that must be it. Let us hope that there is no more to it than that, for a foolish affair of the heart at this stage would only complicate matters unbearably. I had better hold tight to my heart till the Marquis of Rexdale makes his intentions known, for I would not want to end up like Elizabeth or poor Sarah Henley.

Sleep evaded Halcyon. Restlessly she tossed and turned in her bed. Finally she arose and went over to the window to gaze across the moonlit gardens to the shadowy fields beyond, which in turn stretched out into the distance to meet the undulating hills and the inky sky on the horizon.

A movement, a flutter of white in the shrubbery below, attracted her attention. Someone was out there in the darkness! Another movement in a different area impressed itself on her vision. There was more than one person out there.

As Halcyon watched and her eyes became used to the darkness and managed to penetrate the shadows, she saw Clementine hurrying down one of the little paths. Suddenly a tall dark figure stepped out of the bushes. Lord Peter! Clementine rushed into his arms and was held there tight.

Halcyon smiled to herself. A loving tryst in the moonlight—what could be more natural? And how envious she felt of two people who had been lucky enough to find each other. Involuntarily her thoughts turned to Lord Dray. What would it feel like to be held close in his arms in such a way? Her thoughts jolted a shock through her. Why think of Lord Dray at a moment like this? It was the future Marquis of Rexdale—who should have been in her thoughts!

Guiltily Halcyon turned away from the window. She was fantasizing like a silly giddy miss. How foolish to build a web of romance around every handsome gentleman who swept before her vision! If I but knew what the future Marquis of Rexdale looked like, she justified to herself, no doubt it would be of him that I would dream. Satisfied with this, she returned to bed and was soon asleep.

"Halcyon, what is the matter?" asked Lady Hensham. "You have every appearance of being jittery and upset. These few days in the country were supposed to relax you, and I should have thought that you of all people, having been so accustomed to the country, would have found the visit beneficial."

"I'm sorry, ma'am, that my unease was so apparent. It is merely that the silence, the peace and beauty of the country, have made me mindful of my own home and my dear father. I confess I feel quite homesick." It was only partially an untruth, for Halcyon did sorely miss her father, but she would not have her godmother guess at the turmoil of her thoughts regarding Lord Dray. He is becoming too dear to me, she decided, and I must make every effort to hide my feelings—nay, nip them completely and irrevocably in the bud.

It was hard though, for all around her there were signs and reminders of love. William constantly sought out Sarah Henley, Clemmie and Lord Peter were in love for all the world to see; and the Earl of Winthrop carefully but rather unobtrusively avoided Miss Henley.

"Well, child, you had better try to put on a smile, for we cannot have Lord Peter assuming that you are not a contented guest. I hear that there is a croquet party on the lawns; why don't you go out and join it?" advised Lady Hensham.

"Just what I was about to suggest myself," said Lord Winthrop, coming upon them at this moment. "Would you care to accompany me, Miss Glaybourne?"

She could hardly refuse, and yet she knew that Lord Dray would only be more furious.

Wasn't that what she wanted, though? To anger him would make him despise her with a contempt so strong that he would treat her with that cold disdain that certainly allowed no friendship between them. It was the easiest and surest way to protect her foolish heart.

"Why, that would be delightful, Lord Winthrop," she responded with a bright smile.

On the lawn the immaculately dressed Lord Dray could be seen talking to Clementine and Lord Peter, whilst various other groups stood bantering with each other or choosing their mallets and the color of their croquet balls.

"Come and join us," called Clemmie as soon as she saw Halcyon with her escort. "Emma is joining us, too, so that will make up the number evenly." Then, as Halcyon reached her side, she whispered in a voice that carried quite clearly to Lord Dray, who stood not two paces away, "Really, dear, you'll have to be

138

more careful about being seen too often in Lord Winthrop's company, or the whole world will know your secret."

What an infuriating person she was! Halcyon bit her lip. Clemmie would have the rumor all over town if she was not stopped. What mattered even more was the fact that two or three of the other men were now looking at her with speculative interest. If this tale got to the ears of Rexdale's son, she would no doubt be in the suds.

It was bad enough that Lord Dray was tight-lipped and furious, scarcely able to address her, let alone play a decent game under the pressure of the misapprehensions nurtured by Clemmie's indiscretion. He swung his mallet erratically, and even at one point hit the wooden ball with such a thwack that it split asunder.

There were calls of amusement and friendly derision:

"Well played!"

"What a shot!"

"Lord Dray is off his stroke today! Steady on, old man, it's only a game!"

After that he settled down and played in a clipped, decisive way. He contented himself with a supercilious smile of derision whenever Halcyon played a stroke, thus completely turning the tables—now it was she who was anxious and dismayed.

She took an unconscionable number of strokes to finish the game, and, after it was all over, escaped with as much decorum as possible to cool her fiery cheeks.

She ran to the rose garden and agitatedly paced

between the rows of flowers. Really! The man was insufferable!

She whirled around as she heard a step behind her, although she did not need the evidence of her eyes to know who had followed her.

"What on earth was that all about?" she blazed, her caution and decorum thrown to the winds. "I suppose you think that was funny, don't you? Well, let me tell you what *I* think it was. Outrageous, despicable, and—and—ungentlemanly!"

His eyes glinted as he advanced upon her, and she found herself backing away from him in a most cowardly fashion. He seemed to be enjoying the situation, although vestiges of his anger still remained.

"My dear Miss Glaybourne, you must be fair! You have done nothing but tease and humiliate me since last evening. Can you wonder that I paid you back in like coinage?"

"W-what do you mean? Tease and humiliate you? I did no such thing! How ever can you make such a preposterous statement? Upon what evidence do you base your accusations?"

"Why, on the evidence of my own eyes and ears," he almost sneered, and Halcyon wondered fleetingly how she could have ever found him attractive. He was high-handed and domineering—all the things most undesirable in a man. She took another step back, but he only continued to advance. "Can you deny that, in an outrageous lapse of propriety, you went out alone into the garden with the Earl of Winthrop and flirted with him?" Dray's voice was low and clipped, as though he controlled with difficulty some fiercely churning emotion. "Admit it; you and

140

he have met before this weekend, and have been carrying on—"

"How dare you, sir!"

"Do you deny it?"

"I most emphatically do!"

"Then what causes the guilty flush on your cheeks, Miss Glaybourne?"

"That's n-not guilt, it is anger at your—your impudence!"

"Impudence, you call it? I don't suppose you hurled such insults at Lord Winthrop in the garden. What did you do out there? Your cheeks were mightily flushed when you came back in. Has nobody ever told you the dangers of walking alone in the shrubbery with a man in the darkness of night?"

"Don't be ridiculous! What could happen?" she asked naïvely. "I assure you, Lord Dray, that I am perfectly able to take care of myself." The very idea was silly. As if she would have permitted any indelicacies!

"You think so? What a babe you are, Halcyon. And what a fool, to deny your vunerability." Too late she saw the menace in his eyes. Too late she realized that he had backed her into the density of the shrubbery, where the thick foliage protected them from the prying eyes of the house.

His hands shot out and gripped her shoulders, making her cry out.

"Nobody will hear your cries," he told her with a grin.

She struggled ineffectually in his iron hold. She tried to kick out at him, but, divining her intention, he pulled her off balance and held her powerless, half-reclining in his arms.

"What's good for the Earl of Winthrop is good for me too," he said before his mouth swooped down and covered hers.

It was a hard kiss, a cruel kiss, a taking without any giving. When he finally released her and stood away from her, Halcyon could only stand trembling, pale, her beautiful green eyes dulled with dismay.

Dray was breathing heavily, and there was something akin to remorse in his eyes.

"Don't ever presume that you can handle a risky situation," he ground out. "I could have had my way with you, as could Winthrop or any other man with whom you would be foolish enough to wander alone in a secluded place." He turned abruptly on his heel and was gone.

I hate him, I hate him, I hate him! she repeated to herself as she sped to the sanctuary of her room. I hate him! But she didn't. No, it was quite the reverse.

What foolish mess is this? she asked herself in dismay. How have I got myself into such a pickle? Oh, if I had only accepted with willingness and alacrity the news of my betrothal to the future Marquis of Rexdale, Lady Hensham and dear Papa would not have sought to give me a little freedom first. They meant it kindly, but it was the worst thing they could have done for me. And now see how I have betrayed them all!

She just could not face going down and mingling with the guests for the rest of the day. She determined to stay in her room and try to sort some sense out of her tangled emotions.

"You're sure it's merely a headache?" enquired Lady Hensham, concerned that Halcyon had professed herself indisposed.

"Yes, really, Godmother. Don't worry; it's not too bad, but I deemed it wiser to rest now and recover sufficiently to attend the masked ball this evening."

"Very well. I shall have a light lunch sent up to you. Emily, soak a handkerchief in cologne and place it on Miss Halcyon's brow; I always find that works wonders."

Halcyon was glad to be alone. She wanted to think. In spite of Lord Dray's most recent actions—which had hardly done him credit—Halcyon had to admit that, with his flashing silvery gray eyes, his laughing smile, and his superbly dignified air, he had quite captivated her heart. It was something that had come upon her unawares. Her heart had been captured before she had had a chance to defend it.

But, surely, the greatest damage had not yet been done. The earl really rather despised her now—although she felt sure that there had been a brief time when he had liked her enormously—and all she had to do was to smother her feelings of affection and to constantly remind herself that she was promised to another gentleman. It would not be easy. She would suffer dreadfully if she had to see Lord Dray every day and yet know that she harbored a hopeless love for him. Yet she had only herself to blame. This is what came of living a lie, she admonished herself, for was it not a lie to conceal the fact that she was already promised to the Marquis of Rexdale's son? Had he been aware of that fact, Halcyon felt certain that Lord Dray would not have spent so much time in her company, would not have misconstrued her walk in the gardens with Lord Winthrop, and, above all, would not have inflicted on her that punishing kiss.

Her cheeks flamed at the mere memory of it. How could he have done such a thing? It had not been at all like that first kiss he had laughingly snatched; it had been more pain than pleasure, more insult than compliment. Why, he had acted like a man in the grip of a jealous rage. Jealous? Could it be . . . could it possibly be that Lord Dray was jealous? Oh, no! Not possible, surely. For to feel jealousy he would also have to feel love. The thought made Halcyon tremble. If only he did! How deliriously happy she would be.

No, no, no! Not happy! That would be the worst thing of all, for there was no way she could ever hope to turn her back on her duty, break her father's promise, and refuse to marry Lord Rexdale. What had to be, had to be.

Besides, it was nonsense to imagine that Lord Dray entertained any romantic notions about her. She was merely thinking what she wanted to think. The cold, stark reality was that Dray was a little put out by her long absence in the garden with Lord Winthrop . . . a touch of rivalry between two friends . . . Everybody knew that men were like that.

Halcyon sighed. The next days would be long. She almost wished that she had never come to Bath. The tempting idea occurred to her that she could leave the city and return to her father's house; at least there she would be safely out of the way of Lord Dray, and the devastating effect he had on her.

The coward's way out. Halcyon smiled to herself. A solution that would offend her godmother, who had shown her nothing but kindness. Halcyon could not do that to Lady Hensham. It was not her fault that her little plan to allow her goddaughter to have a small measure of freedom and harmless amusement had turned about. No, Halcyon would just have to put on a brave face.

CHAPTER ELEVEN

Dressed in a vivid scarlet oriental robe, her golden-red hair hidden by a black wig, and the greater part of her face concealed under an ornate white satin mask, Halcyon felt sure that she was virtually unrecognizable.

The ball was being held in the huge entrance hall of Brampton Court. As she descended the wide staircase, Halcyon drew in her breath in delight. The gleaming chandeliers had been lit, and they cast a flickering glow over the scene below.

The servants must have been working all day to achieve such a transformation. Large baskets of flowers had been placed around the hall, and their sweetness floated delicately, tantalizingly, up to where Halcyon stood. It had surely taken skill and imagination to wind the blossom-laden branches through the railings of the gallery overhead.

At the far end of the gallery, playing like a heavenly host, several musicians had been installed.

As Halcyon came further down the stairs, she saw that the double doors of the dining room were open wide, revealing tables piled high with assorted delicacies.

Much as she dreaded meeting with Lord Dray again, her anxiety was relieved by the knowledge that she was well and truly hidden by her mask. Which of the gentlemen was he? she wondered. Most of them wore, besides their masks, powdered wigs that concealed their own hair, by which they might have been identified. Some of the figures could be easily ruled out. One of the gentlemen was much too short, another too plump—that must be Lord Henley—and still another walked with a slouch.

She knew Clemmie immediately. As the host, Lord Peter had not worn a mask, and standing beside him was Clementine, dressed in palest blue satin in Marie Antoinette style, and wearing a white high-piled wig.

"Save the first dance for me," whispered a voice in her ear. It was a voice she recognized.

Turning quickly, she beheld a magnificent figure dressed in a white satin shirt with wide blouson sleeves caught tight at the wrists, tight black satin breeches, knee boots with silver buckles, and a purple cummerbund around his waist. He sported a small black moustache, his hair covered by a purple scarf, and he wore a patch over one eye.

Halcyon gasped in astonishment. "You look fearsome! I would not have recognized you, my lord. But how did you know me?" she cried in disappointment. "I felt sure I had a secure disguise."

"How could I mistake you?" he laughed, leading her on to the floor for the first dance. "Who else comes just up to my heart?" he whispered.

It seemed he had forgotten their earlier dissension —or at least chosen to ignore it—and as a result Halcyon lost her anxiety and began to thoroughly enjoy the evening.

She danced several more times with him, twice with Lord Peter Brampton, and once with Lord

Charles Winthrop—for by this time even the most difficult disguises had been penetrated.

The atmosphere became hot and stifling in the hall as the evening progressed, and the huge entrance doors and the floor-length windows on either side were thrown open to the night air.

Seeing her cast several longing looks outside, Lord Charles, who was her partner at that time, suggested that they might take a stroll in the garden. She gracefully declined without giving a reason, since she knew that to repeat the incident that had angered Dray in the first place would be foolhardy.

All the same, she sighed, she would like to breathe in some fresh air. Perhaps later . . .

The opportunity came earlier than she had expected. At the end of the dance Lord Winthrop was called away and she found herself momentarily without a partner. Surely nobody would notice if she simply slipped out by herself.

The stars sprinkled the vault of heaven with diamond lights. The night was soft, clear, and still. Only the faintest whisper of a breeze could be heard murmuring to the leaves like a soft-tongued lover.

Halcyon made her way across the lawns and through the shrubbery. Beyond this was a grove of trees where she had discovered a stone bench under a giant beech. She sat down, spreading her dress so that it would not snag on the rough surface. The trouble with pretty clothes, she decided, was that one had to be so careful of them. She thought back longingly to the days when she had roamed so carefree in her father's woods, never bothering when her dress had been caught by the snagging briers, paying no heed to the twigs and the stones in her path, unmindful of anything save the acute, exquisite joy of being young and free under the smiling sky that bountifully displayed a thousand delights to her.

She remembered the deer in the meadows, and the lovely little fawn that had trustingly bent to nuzzle her face; the rabbits that would seem to play hide-and-seek with each other in the dappled sunlight as they raced across the fields; the birds, the scurrying creatures of the underbrush, the flowers.

Suddenly she was homesick with the agony of a longing that rose in her throat and cut her breath into jagged rasps. Oh, to be home again! She leaned back against the ragged bark of the tree and closed her eyes. Home!

She felt her tears welling up behind her closed eyelids till she had to blink and let them brim over. How ridiculous to feel so despondent, so lost.

A dark form detached itself from the shadows.

"Halcyon! What ever is the matter?" Strong but gentle hands took hold of hers as Lord Dray sat down beside her on the stone bench.

Quickly Halcyon dashed away the feminine weakness of tears before raising limpid eyes to his.

"N-nothing is the matter, my lord," she lied. "What gave you that idea?"

He regarded her searchingly, and she knew she had not fooled him.

"You were feeling sad," he exclaimed, "and I very much suspect that was my fault."

"Oh no, not at all! I—I was thinking of home, you see. Of Papa, and the woods, the flower-scattered fields, the evening sun sinking over the distant hills. Oh, how I long to be back!"

"You don't enjoy the mad social whirl of Bath, then? The balls, the *thés*, the parties?"

"Of course I do. They are a novelty. But, you see, that's just what they are—a novelty. To me they are not a way of life; I don't take them seriously, as does everyone else here. They are an unnecessary frivolity, as unsubstantial as a rainbow after a quick summer shower. I don't fit in to this life, my lord."

It was easy to talk to him in the anonymity of the darkness. She had bottled up these feelings and now they were spilling out. She rebelled against the fake, the sham of the society people and their pastimes, the glitter, excitement, and abundance that was on the surface masking the other, not-so-pleasant things underneath—the loveless reality of an arranged marriage, the mating of a young girl to a gouty old man as was Elizabeth's lot, the pairing off of young people for money or titles instead of for love. It all tumbled out of her. She talked as if she would never stop, and all the while Dray held her hand in his and listened.

"Halcyon, my love," he said finally, "what a tenderhearted rebel you are! I suspect you feel everything too strongly; you probably want to champion the whole world! You should have been a man in the times of knights and dragons, instead of which you are just a child—No! I am wrong. Only half of you is a child, for the other half is a charming, beguiling woman, a woman who has a most strangely bewitching effect on me." He pulled her gently to her feet and held her close. "I wonder if you can imagine how I feel about you?"

Halcyon almost swooned with delight and yearning. She had been right, after all! His anger earlier in the day had been promoted by jealousy. He did love her! Oh, she could stay like this in the circle of his arms forever. What more could she ask of life than Dray's love? This was all she had ever wanted, all she had ever dreamed of, this was . . .

Madness! She must not allow this to happen! Her heart might rebel, but her duty was plain. What she did now would rule the rest of her life. Since she had to marry the future Marquis of Rexdale and live with him as his wife, she would not betray him before she had even met him. She must be strong. She must never, never allow Dray to suspect that she returned his affection.

"Halcyon, my love." His voice was soft and wooing. His hand lifted her chin so that her face was upturned to his. He kissed her forehead, her closed eyelids. Oh, the heaven of it!

But no . . . no. She struggled. Her arms strained to push him away.

"No! Unhand me, my lord!"

"What is amiss?"

"You presume too much!"

"How so? I love you, Halcyon. I felt sure my feelings were reciprocated!" His brow creased in puzzlement.

"You were mistaken." Her eyes were downcast. She could not look at him.

"I don't believe it! Look at me! Tell me again!"

She raised her liquid gaze to his. She forced her mind and her heart to detach themselves from what she was saying. She had to convince him, for she knew that his zealous pursuit of her would cast asunder all her defenses.

"I don't love you! I love another!"

"Dammit! You do, do you?" He hurled her away

from him. "Then I was right! There *is* something between you and Charles!"

"No!" Alarm laced her voice. "Not him!"

"Who, then?"

"I cannot tell you. I see no reason to tell you, my lord."

He was still not totally convinced.

"But just now I could have sworn that you—dash it all! You confided in me. I felt sure—"

"It was nothing more than a vunerable, despondent moment. Pray do not read too much into it. And if you really bear me any affection, my lord, you can best show it by not harassing me further."

"Harass—! Egad! Is that how you look upon it? Fie, Miss Glaybourne! I have twice rescued you from perilous situations—do you construe that as harassment?"

"Believe me, I was grateful for your aid on those occasions, but do you expect limitless gratitude?" She strove to make her voice indifferent.

"My abject apologies, ma'am." He bowed briefly. His steely eyes cut through her. "You shall not find that fault in me again."

CHAPTER TWELVE

"My dear Elizabeth!" Halcyon rose to greet her friend. "Do come in! Have you been long in Bath? You could not have arrived at a more opportune time, since my godmother is visiting Lady Cranshaw this morning and we may thus enjoy a cozy chat undisturbed."

"Hmmm. You are looking pale, Halcyon," commented Elizabeth as soon as she had embraced her. "Can it be that the Bath air does not agree with you? Strange, for they say that it is the most salubrious in the whole of the country."

"It is nothing. I have been a trifle indisposed. But let us not waste time in pleasantries. My dear, I must tell you, I have met the Earl of Winthrop."

An eager flush rose to Elizabeth's cheeks.

"Indeed? Oh, Halcyon, tell me how it is with him? Did you speak with him? Did he mention me? Oh, I have been so agitated for news of him!"

"Now calm yourself, and I will tell you all. You are not aware, I am sure, that I recently had the pleasure of attending a houseparty at the Earl of Brampton's estate. Did you hear that he has spoken for Clementine Cranshaw? Well, to get back to my story, Lord Dray introduced me to your Lord Winthrop. I had not realized that they were friends."

"Lord Dray?" asked Elizabeth in some puzzlement. "You mean that you . . . well, never mind. Go on."

"I had no sooner intimated to Lord Winthrop that I was friendly with you than he immediately bore me off to talk of you. He said he suspected that the dismissal of your maid had been caused by the suspicion that she was carrying notes between the two of you."

Elizabeth nodded.

"And most concerned about it he was, too. In fact, he asked me to try to arrange a meeting between you as soon as you arrived in Bath."

"Oh, he wants to see me? Does he know that we are accompanied here by Lord Medford?"

"I acquainted him with that fact."

"Then he must surely be aware of the impossibility of our meeting."

"Naturally. I did not promise anything, Elizabeth, for I felt bound to seek your opinion first. I would not blame you if you were to decide—"

"My dear, there is no decision. Had I stopped sooner in this madness, there would have been a possibility of rational choice, but I fear I am completely lost. I love Charles, Halcyon. I truly do, and to be deprived of the joy of being with him—even if it is rarely and briefly—is not to be endured. You will help us, won't you? Nobody will suspect an ulterior motive in my visits with you."

Halcyon stared at her and slowly nodded.

"I cannot pretend that I think it is wise . . . but, yes, I will help you."

"Thank you. Thank you. You are a true friend! And now, tell me, what do you think of Lord Dray?"

"Lord Dray? Why should I think anything of

him?" Halcyon attempted to keep the lilt out of her voice. "He is adequately charming, handsome, dances well—but then so do a dozen others, Elizabeth. I cannot think of any reason to single out his lordship." She dismissed the subject with a shrug, and after a sharp glance in her direction, Elizabeth allowed her to turn the conversation in another direction.

They planned that Halcyon should call at Lord Winthrop's lodgings in Great Pulteney Street on the morrow and leave with his manservant a note from Elizabeth, informing him that both she and Halcyon would be walking in the Sydney Gardens that afternoon.

"He will be sure to come," decided Elizabeth, "and I shall have an opportunity to talk with him again. By the way, I was instructed by Mama to invite your godmother and you to dinner tomorrow evening. You shall have the unparalleled pleasure of meeting Lord Medford," she added dryly as she took her leave.

It would not do for anyone to see her entering Lord Winthrop's lodgings, decided Halcyon, so she dismissed her carriage at Pulteney Bridge, claiming that she had several errands which would take her upwards of an hour, and that the coach should return for her later.

Then, on foot, she crossed the bridge, which was lined with shops of every description. She would have dearly liked to tarry and examine the goods at leisure, but decided that such pleasurable pursuits could only be enjoyed after she had delivered Elizabeth's note.

Once across the bridge she directed her steps across Laura Place, at the far end of which Great Pulteney Street led to the Sydney Gardens.

It was a fair September day. The summer heat still lingered and Halcyon was dressed in a fine muslin dress over which she had thrown a light pelisse. At this time of the year the weather could be so changeable.

Arrived at Great Pulteney Street, she started to count off the numbers of the houses; it would not do to miss Lord Charles's lodgings and have to retrace her steps and so draw attention to herself.

Elizabeth had impressed on her the necessity of conserving her anonymity, for if anyone saw her they would wonder what she was doing in that area of town and might possibly put two and two together and guess that her visit to Lord Winthrop's lodgings had something to do with Elizabeth.

Personally, Halcyon was not in favour of all this subterfuge; but Elizabeth was her friend and she felt duty bound to help her in any way she could. After all, she argued with herself, it was not as though the young lovers were really doing anything wrong; she was sure that their behavior was always the most circumspect.

She found the number for which she was searching and turned into the entrance.

Lord Winthrop's manservant answered the peal of the bell. No, he informed her, his lordship was not at present in, but he would certainly see that he was given the note the very moment of his return. Would the young lady like to enter and await his lordship and deliver the message in person?

Halcyon assured him that that would not be necessary. She was eager to be on her way, once she was assured Lord Charles would receive the note that afternoon at the very latest.

Then she turned and half-ran out of the building, so anxious to have done with her small part in the subterfuge that she did not look where she was going and collided in the entrance with a tall figure.

"My apologies, ma'am—Halcyon!" Lord Dray could scarcely have been more surprised and dismayed than she herself was. "Miss Glaybourne!" The cynical twist was about his mouth again, Halcyon noted. "May I be so bold as to ask you what you are doing at Lord Winthrop's lodgings?"

"N-nothing." What else could she say? Halcyon was completely at loss for a plausible excuse. How bad this looked after her strong denial that there was no secret liaison between herself and the earl.

"You know what I think, Miss Glaybourne?"

"Yes, I do! I know exactly what you think! But you are wrong!" Her eyes flashed angrily.

"And yet I find you in most incriminating circumstances."

"Circumstances that are incriminating only in your eyes. And now, if you will kindly step out of my path, sir, I should like to be on my way."

"No, wait. Mayhap I should accompany you." He glanced up at the building. "Is Winthrop home?"

"You will have to ascertain that for yourself, my lord. And I require no assistance from you, thank you. It is but a few steps to where my carriage awaits."

"I see." He looked down at her. His mouth was a straight, thin line. Halcyon could have shriveled up under the contempt of his eyes. "Then I bid you good day, Miss Glaybourne."

Why, oh why did Lord Dray always come upon her in the most awkward of situations? Halcyon asked herself as she quickly sped back to Pulteney Bridge. It seemed as if he dogged her very footsteps, and if she were engaged in anything underhand, he would be sure to ferret it out. Well, in this case he had completely the wrong idea. He suspected her of having an affair with Lord Charles; it was laughable, really! Elizabeth's secret could not have been more safe. It was obvious that Lord Dray had got an idea into his head and held on to it with such tenacity that he would not see the truth were it plainly written in front of his very aristocratic nose.

Her encounter with Dray had delayed her more than she had expected, and there was therefore no time for her to shop before lunch. She must return to the house with all speed, for if there was one thing that Lady Hensham hated, it was to be kept waiting for meals. It would not do to put her into a pique just now, today of all days, for she must be in a good humor and agree to Halcyon's outing with Elizabeth that afternoon to the Sydney Gardens. The alarming thought occurred that perhaps her ladyship might wish to accompany them. That would put the cat among the pigeons!

Her fears were groundless. Lady Hensham showed no inclination to accompany them and was quite agreeable to them going by themselves.

"A most pleasant place," she approved. "How often I have strolled between the flowerbeds, taking the air and viewing the fashions. So nice for you girls to have each other for companionship, my dears. And how is Lord Medford, Elizabeth? I hear he accompanied your family to Bath?"

"Yes, aunt. He is well," replied Elizabeth shortly.

"Hmmm. He did not wish to accompany you to the Gardens, then?"

"He did not, ma'am. In fact, his gout was troubling him, and I believe he is taking the waters at the Pump Room." If Elizabeth's scorn was ill disguised, Lady Hensham made no comment.

"Off you go then. Do not be late in returning, Halcyon my dear, for we are dining with Sir Henry."

"Does he really have gout?" asked Halcyon when they were rolling through the streets of Bath in the carriage.

"Among other things." Elizabeth made a moue of distaste. "Just wait till you meet him tonight, Halcyon. You will scarcely credit the evidence of your own eyes. Oh, I know I should not speak so badly of him, but I confess that I find it ever harder to conceal my disgust. I must marry him, for if I do not, poor Papa faces certain ruin. I could not live with that. If I only had not met the Earl of Winthrop, I am sure that I would have found my fate so much easier to bear. If I had never known love, perhaps I would not have set such great store by it. Oh, what a quandary I am in! Do you suppose the earl will be able to meet us in the Gardens? Did you speak with him in person, Halcyon?"

"No, I have been waiting for an opportunity to speak with you. I gave the note to his manservant, who assured me that his lordship should have it immediately upon his return. We must simply hope that he returns in time to make the rendezvous."

She said nothing of her encounter with Lord Anthony Dray. There was very little to be gained by worrying Elizabeth still further. If Dray caused any trouble, it would surely be with herself or with Lord Charles. Strange that the earl had not told Dray of his secret amour. After all, they were friends, were they not?

There were many people in the Gardens. Several ladies and gentlemen strolled the paths, walking arm in arm; families enjoyed relaxation in the fresh air, the parents walking ahead of children in the care of nursemaids. The flower beds were a colorful splash amidst the wide swathes of greenery.

Elizabeth stared eagerly around her.

"I wonder if he is here yet. We must have the carriage wait for us here, Halcyon. After we have walked for a time, we shall take some tea before returning home. I do hope he is here."

Fortunately the earl joined them very shortly, and Elizabeth was in the seventh heaven.

"I can never thank you enough, Miss Glaybourne," said the earl, "for arranging this meeting between Elizabeth and myself. I was beginning to lose hope of ever seeing her again alone. And how kind of you to accompany her here, for thus our secret could not be more safe. If anyone sees us, they will assume a chance meeting, or they will believe that my interest is in you."

It was this latter of which Halcyon was more particularly afraid. All she needed now, she reflected wryly, was for Earl Dray to appear from nowhere. After all, he had a habit of popping up just where he was least needed!

So she was hardly surprised when, after walking back and forth for an hour and then repairing to the

Tea House for refreshment, she saw Lord Dray on the outskirts of the crowd.

I do believe he has been following me, she decided with chagrin, for it seemed too much of a coincidence for him to have casually come upon her yet again.

Lord Charles had seen him, too.

"Come over here and join us, Tony," he exclaimed imperturbably. If the fact that Dray had seen them mattered so little, why did Winthrop not tell his friend the truth? wondered Halcyon crossly. The earl might be calm about the whole matter, but she was decidedly flustered. As his lordship came up to them, she could feel the unwanted color rising to flood her cheeks, and she could scarcely meet his eyes when he greeted her.

He consented to partake of some tea with them, and whilst Charles and Elizabeth were deep in a conversation of their own, he murmured to her, "Very clever, Miss Glaybourne. You have my admiration."

"W-what ever do you mean?" she stammered.

"Mean? Why, what else would I mean than the adroit way in which you have set this up. It would appear for all the world as if Lord Charles and your friend Elizabeth were enjoying a secret meeting. How well you have masked the real situation!"

"Indeed?" She hoped her voice was a cold as his eyes. "How very discerning you are, my lord. But I would ask you one question: how can you be sure that it is not the other way around? That I am not the decoy for Elizabeth?"

Dray threw back his head and laughed. "An admirable attempt. But if that were the case, would not the earl be now chatting ardently with you in order to lead one's suspicions away from Miss Cecil? Oh, no, it is perfectly clear to me what is happening here."

"Even if you are right," Halcyon was stung into retorting, "why do you condemn what you see? Is it so wrong to seek out the company of those we love?"

"Of course not. And it is not that which I condemn. It is the lie you told me. I would have understood if you had admitted that you were in love with Charles—nay. more than that, I should have helped you. But careful; Charles is rather doubtfully regarding us."

"What are you two discussing so earnestly?" asked Elizabeth. "You look for all the world like a pair of conspirators."

"I was merely suggesting," replied Lord Dray smoothly, "that I should drive Miss Halcyon back to the Crescent in my gig. That will leave Lord Charles free to return you to your house, Miss Cecil."

"No, no, that will not do at all," burst out Elizabeth. Then she bit her lip, fearing she had given herself away.

However, his lordship placed his own construction on her dilemma, smiling triumphantly at Halcyon as though to say: See, I told you so; she would not split up you and the earl! "On second thought," he said, "I had better not interfere in your arrangements, for I have a meeting of my own shortly."

"Do you think he guessed?" asked Elizabeth anxiously as they were returning in the carriage.

"I'm sure nothing could be further from his mind," Halcyon assured her in positive tones. "Believe me, Elizabeth, Lord Dray will be the last one to uncover your secret," she added bitterly.

Halcyon was beginning to heartily regret her part in this tangle of deceit, and was on the verge of confessing to her friend that she could no longer continue with the subterfuge. She would speak to Elizabeth after dinner, she decided.

However, after meeting Lord Medford, she changed her mind.

What a horrible creature he was! Halcyon gazed at him wide-eyed and shocked. How could Elizabeth, a young girl, full of youth and beauty and life, be expected to marry such an ogre? He was fat and ugly and at least fifty years old! True, he was clothed in expensive satin of the very best cut, his pudgy fingers were laden with flashing rings, and Halcyon was sure that the buttons on his waistcoat were real diamonds. But his hair was unfashionably long and was greasy as though too infrequently washed.

What could Sir Henry be thinking of to marry off his eldest daughter to such a man?

She knew the answer to that, of course. Those diamond buttons blinked the answer to her.

Poor, poor Elizabeth. And how could Halcyon deny her the comparatively small pleasure of a few innocent hours spent with the Earl of Winthrop? She would soon enough have to pay for those happy hours.

Sir Henry must be in well over his head. Lord Medford was staying at the Cecils' town house. But Elizabeth had intimated that it wasn't her father who was paying the shot, that it was indeed the wealthy suitor who was the real host in her own father's house.

A strange state of affairs. How had Sir Henry

come to this? Halcyon wondered. Of course, it was not unusual for a man to lose his fortune at the tables, but was Sir Henry a gambler?

Her intention to extricate herself from the dubious task of go-between for Elizabeth and her earl thus thwarted, Halcyon had no choice but to continue arranging meetings and passing notes between the two of them.

There were, admittedly, times when she felt that they were taking far too much for granted and implicating her more than they implicated themselves, but Halcyon made excuses for them, feeling that love was indeed blind; they had no eyes or thoughts for anyone but themselves.

CHAPTER THIRTEEN

Halcyon was returning from delivering a note to Lord Charles. She had dismissed the carriage, feeling in the need for some air and a few minutes to herself.

She knew it was incautious for her to make her way through the back streets as she had on that other occasion that had so very nearly ended in disaster, but on this day she was feeling faint-hearted and despondent.

She had not seen Lord Dray for several days; indeed he was no longer a frequent visitor to the house on the Crescent. Even Lady Hensham had commented on his lengthy absence, fixing a reprimanding stare on Halcyon and asking whether her goddaughter knew of any reason why his lordship should be deliberately avoiding them.

Halcyon had blushed but remained silent. There was nothing she could tell her godmother. If that good lady had any questions, she should pose them to the earl himself. After all, it was she in the first place who had encouraged Dray to call at the house and had positively foisted Halcyon off on him.

Had she been wise to deliberately allow him to think the worst of her? Had she been wise to discourage his attentions? She could have been like Elizabeth, enjoying a last-minute fling before her wings were cut. Would that have been so very bad?

Halcyon's brow creased in dismay. She saw all too

clearly what was happening between Elizabeth and the earl. They were becoming all too dependent on their stolen meetings. They were like two people on a runaway toboggan sliding downhill and fast gathering speed. She was afraid that soon they would be out of control, beyond reason.

She was so lost in these thoughts that at first she did not notice the small boy trailing along at her side. When she did finally become aware of him, she stopped still in amazement.

"Why, you're the lad who defended me from those thieves!" she exclaimed.

"Yes, miss," he agreed.

"How glad I am to have an opportunity to thank you. You can't imagine how worried I was about you that day—you ran off before I had a chance to see the extent of that wound on your head. Is it quite healed?"

"Quite well, miss, though it does throb something terrible at times."

"You speak well for a beggar boy," she couldn't help remarking.

"I ain't a beggar, miss."

"Oh! I—I thought . . ."

"You thought I was agoin' to steal your reticule, too, didn't yer, miss?"

Halcyon regarded him with a slight smile. "Well, yes, now you mention it," she admitted, "the thought did cross my mind. What's your name, boy?"

"Samuel, miss. They calls me Sammy at home."

"I see." What an engaging fellow he was. "And just where is home, Sammy?"

"Down yonder." He pointed to a maze of twisting streets that led down to the walls of the city. "Me mum lives there with ten of us young 'uns. Though she says we won't be there for much longer if we doesn't pay the rent."

"What does your father do?" Ten youngsters! It must be hard to make ends meet.

"Me father left us, and me mother's too sick to work just now. She's expecting another little 'un any day now, and she's been proper poorly. Don't suppose yer knows of any work for me, miss?"

"Oh Sammy!" Halcyon stared at him in dismay. "If only I did! Are things really that bad at home?"

He nodded mutely.

"Then I must try to help you," she decided. It wrung her heart to see poverty of any sort, but this little fellow was especially appealing. Perhaps she would at least be able to make his mother more comfortable. "Take me to your home."

"Now, miss?" he asked in surprise.

"Right this minute."

"But—but it ain't the place for a lady, miss."

"Take me there."

The house was rundown and dilapidated, but clean and tidy in a pathetically sparse fashion.

Sammy's mother lay on a makeshift bed in one corner of the living room, her eyes too bright and her color yellow and waxen.

"Sam's a good boy," was all she said when Halcyon explained that Sam had brought her to see if she could be of any help. Her breathing was shallow and rapid, and Halcyon knew at once that she needed medication and the services of a doctor. Hastily she reached into her reticule.

"Now here, take this, Sammy." She handed him some money, but he refused to accept it.

"I ain't looking for handouts, miss," he told her.

"Don't be silly, it's not a handout. You'll be working for this. Now, listen carefully. Every day at precisely ten in the morning you will come to the servants' entrance of Lady Hensham's house in the Royal Crescent. Do you understand? Then you will ask for Rebecca Parkes; she will like as not have an errand for you to run. You must do as she says and never tell anyone what you are about."

"Very well, miss." He was grinning at her amiably.

"And this afternoon I shall have some medication sent to your mother. Make sure that she takes it."

"Lawks, miss, you didn't have to use the boy for messenger. You knows I would run notes back and forth between Miss Elizabeth and her beau!"

"I know that, Rebecca. At first I preferred to go myself, so as not to arouse suspicion, for everyone knows that a lady's maid is often used as a go-between. But the task is now becoming onerous, and I fear that my godmother is becoming suspicious over my frequent absence from the house. Besides, the lad, Sammy, needs money quite desperately. His mother is sick and I believe the father has deserted them."

Rebecca nodded sympathetically.

"I knows the story, miss. What does you want him to do?"

"He will run between Miss Elizabeth and Lord Charles, picking up and delivering notes. I can tell you that he will be kept trotting, for I myself am just about worn to a frazzle with the volume of communication that goes on between those two," she added with some humor. "First thing in the morning you will send him to Miss Elizabeth's with a letter that I shall write explaining all to her."

"Very well, miss. Anything else, miss?"

"Yes." Halcyon went over to her jewelry box and selected a ruby pendant set in gold filigree. "This used to belong to my mother. It is one of the few valuable things I own." She gave one last look at it before handing it to her maid. "Rebecca, I want you to take this to the pawnbroker's. Get as much as you can for it. Then I want you to search out the services of a doctor, one who will not mind venturing down into the poorer part of town. He is to go to the last alley off Southgate Street before the city walls. There's a rundown house, several children playing in the dirt outside. The mother is sick and expecting a child any day now. He must see what can be done for her."

"Yes, miss." Rebecca gaped at her in amazement. "But are you sure you knows what you're doing?"

"Yes. Now, pray go quickly, for it seemed to me that the woman was very sick."

Sammy's assistance proved to be a blessing. Always of a sunny disposition and unfailingly willing to offer his untiring services, he soon made it possible for Halcyon to resume her normal activities and leave Elizabeth's stream of passionate letters to the Earl in his capable hands.

He well understood the urgent need for secrecy, and Halcyon was aware that in him she had found a trustworthy servant. He professed himself undyingly grateful for Halcyon's aid to his mother, imparting the news that she now fared much better; the doctor had seen her, had left explicit instructions for her care, and the medicament prescribed had done no end of good. It merely remained now for the tardy baby to make an appearance, and his mother would be able to resume the normal tasks and duties of life.

Not only was she glad of Sammy's help in the matter with Elizabeth, but Halcyon also had been delighted to be of aid to the boy and his family. It irked her to think that some people were born into this life with an intolerable burden to bear. Although by no means a lady of fortune herself, she had nevertheless never found herself in the dire need and abject misery that Sammy had known all his life. If she could do but some small thing to relieve it, she was happy.

In other areas her life did not run quite as smoothly. She had had various encounters with Dray—once in the Pump Room, twice in the bustling streets of Bath, and yet another time at a *thé* given by the Countess of Westmorland. On each occasion he had been civil, but coolly so, never addressing to her more than the barest minimum of words required by common decency. She knew she had angered him; it irked her sorely to think that he would suspect her of a clandestine affair with Winthrop, but, in the interests of keeping Elizabeth's secret, Halcyon was powerless to make explanations and so absolve herself in Lord Dray's eyes. One day, she told herself, Winthrop, who is after all his friend, will tell him the whole matter and he will then understand.

But this thought was of very little consolation. After all, what did it matter what Lord Anthony Dray thought of her? Did she want his good opinion? Did she want his love? Yes, yes! cried her foolish heart, whilst her head struggled to enforce reality and practicality by reminding her that to be assured of his love would only render all the more painful the fact that she must perforce marry the future Marquis of Rexdale. 'Tis better that he should think ill of me, she told herself, for in that way there can be no temptation for me to shirk my duty. Why, I should then be in the very same pickle as Elizabeth now finds herself torn between love and duty, and happy with neither.

With these confusing thoughts in mind, Halcyon returned one day to the Crescent from a visit to Clementine Cranshaw's. To her surprise, she found Lord Dray awaiting her. Surprised that, after so long an absence and so dedicated an avoidance of her, he should now be anxious to see her, she greeted him rather coolly.

"Good morning, my lord. Are you waiting to see my godmother? I fear that you have come on an empty quest, for she is with her *modiste* till lunch."

"It is you I came to see, Miss Glaybourne." As he looked at her, the full force of his dislike hit her like a physical blow.

"Really?" Eyebrows raised, she waited for him to continue. He showed no signs of doing this and she was forced to add, "And what, pray, might I do for you?"

"It is not what you might do for me, Miss Glaybourne, but rather what I have done for you." His fists had been clenched at his sides, but now he opened one of them, almost defiantly displaying what he had hidden there. "I believe this pendant belongs to you?" The gold-filigree pendant with the ruby winked up at her from his palm.

"W-where did you get that?" she asked faintly.

"Where you left it, Miss Glaybourne. In the Pump Room last week you opened your reticule for a handkerchief and the pawn ticket fell out. I hope you will forgive me for not returning it to you at once, but I'm afraid my curiosity got the better of me." His voice was sarcastic. "Have you—can you really have stooped so low? Is it not enough to flagrantly carry on an affair with Winthrop? Have you resorted to buying his favors by pawning your jewels?" His lips curled into a sneer.

"How dare you! How *dare* you!" She was white with anger. "How is it that you misconstrue everything you see? Oh, I pity you, Lord Dray! I pity the bitterness of your twisted soul, that finds only ugliness where beauty reigns! When you look at a rose, my lord, do you see only the greenfly? Is your vision of a summer's day marred by the clouds?"

"Well spoken, Miss Glaybourne! Fine sentiments —a surprise coming from you, of all people!"

What bitterness was in the man's heart to so blind him to the truth? Whatever she did, she would be wrong in his eyes. There was no point in trying to vindicate herself or in making any explanations.

"Thank you for the pendant," she said stiffly. "An unnecessary act of chivalry." Only it hadn't been chivalry—they both knew that; he had merely wanted to throw it in her face and shame her with his accusations. "Pray excuse me, I have other things to do. Pray feel free to await my godmother, if you so desire." She swept from the room without waiting to see his reaction.

She had conducted herself commendably throughout the stressful interview, she told herself as she hurried to her room. She maintained her calm until she had reached the sanctuary of its four walls, and then she sped across the room and flung herself on her bed, to burst into a fit of desolate weeping. Oh, life is indeed cruel, she sobbed to herself. Cruel, cruel, indeed!

"What ever is the matter, miss?" exclaimed Rebecca as she saw the state of her beloved mistress. "Who has been upsetting you now?"

"Oh, Rebecca!" cried Halcyon, sitting up and turning to look at her maid with anguished eyes. "I'm s-so m-miserable!"

"Well, well, well," tutted Rebecca. "Do not carry on so, miss, for there's nothing so bad as it can't be speedily rectified." She produced a lacy scrap from one of the drawers and handed it to Halcyon. "Here, miss, dry your eyes and tell me all about it, for as like as not I shall find a solution for you," she declared. Rebecca was quite sure that her beautiful young mistress, who at first glance appeared to have everything to make life extremely tolerable—beauty, no lack of money, admirers by the score—must be fretting over a mere morsel.

"I fear there is no solution, Rebecca, dear," said Halcyon sorrowfully. "There is nothing that you or anyone else can do that will put matters right." Again she burst into a fresh storm of weeping.

"Here now, here now," remonstrated her abigail. "I'll warrant there must be something we can do. Here, sit on this stool and let me brush your hair"— this was Rebecca's antidote for all ills—"and tell me about it."

"It's no use," sniffed Halcyon. But she sat on the stool nonetheless. "It is all a result of my own foolish, wayward dreams. I should have known better than to place myself in such a position, when I well knew the possible consequences."

"Huh?" Rebecca was mystified. No doubt her mistress knew what she was talking about, but it was all double dutch to her.

"You see," explained Halcyon, noting her confusion, "I have fallen in love."

Rebecca's brow cleared. "Is that all?" She beamed. "Well, why didn't you say so in the first place? That ain't no difficulty, miss; it 'appens all the time. Now, do tell, who is the lucky gent?"

"But you fail to understand! I am already promised to another. How can I be in love with one and turn my face away to regard my future as the wife of another? Oh, intolerable thought! If only I had never come to Bath; if only I had never met Lord Dray! If only my father had not already promised me to the Marquis of Rexdale's son!"

"Best tell me it all." Rebecca was now fully aware of the gravity of the situation. "Let me see, do I have this right? You love Lord Dray, miss?"

Halcyon nodded mutely.

"And he loves you?"

"Oh, no!" Halcyon wailed. "H-he despises me! He thinks I am even now busily engaged in a clandestine affair with his great friend Lord Winthrop. I cannot tell him Elizabeth's secret. I shall have to bear his scorn and his bitter accusations."

"Hmmm . . . Jealous, is he, miss?"

"He gives every appearance. I can scarcely imagine why."

"Why, miss, 'tis as plain as the nose on your face! He loves you, to be sure!"

"If he is, then it only makes matters worse."

"How so, miss?" Rebecca's brow furrowed in perplexity. "I had thought that to be good news."

"But, you see, Rebecca, I am promised to another. Have I not just told you that my father made a promise to his old friend the Marquis of Rexdale that I should marry his son? I would prefer that Lord Dray hated me; it would be easier to bear if I knew he hated me."

Rebecca sighed. How complicated these people made the simple fact of love. All this talk of duty and honor and promises to be kept. The gentry were to be truly pitied for their lack of insight into the real importance of life. You took what you needed when you needed it, in Rebecca's world. If love offered itself, then you took it gladly, and if it turned out awry, then you accepted that, too. She shrugged her shoulders.

"Well, miss, you can't have it both ways. First you cry because he despises you, then you weep because you fear he loves you. It seems to me that you have to decide what's important to you. Either you love him more than anything else and you marry him, or you sends him packing and marries the little marquis, like your father says. Seems clear to me."

"What would you do, Rebecca, in my circumstances?" asked Halcyon curiously.

"Lawks, miss! Don't ask me that! I ain't had the sort of life you have. Got no father—leastways, I don't remember him, and sure I don't feel no obligation to a man what run off and left my mother with all us young 'uns."

"You'd marry for love?"

"I guess I would." Rebecca nodded.

"In spite of a promise?"

"Miss, how can I explain it to you?" Her abigail sighed. "For the people I comes from there ain't no such thing as promises and obligations. You takes the bad with a smile and you grabs at the good when it comes your way. It's as simple as that."

Halcyon's eyes filled with commiserative tears. "Oh, Rebecca, what a selfish wretch I am. I have had such a good life; I have been loved and cared for, and the promise made by my father to the Marquis of Rexdale was more for my benefit than for anyone else's. Compared to you . . . oh, my dear! What a dreadful time you must have had as a child! And here am I complaining and weeping over a trifle. I owe my father everything. My godmother, too, has been so good to me. I lack for nothing. She showers me with gifts and I know that it is her money that is being lavished on me now." She dried her tears. "Thank you, Rebecca, for making me see the folly of my ways."

"Glad to be of service, miss," smiled her maid as she left the room.

Halcyon was once more alone. She knew what she had to do. She had known it all along, so why did she torture herself in this way with all the might-have-beens of life? I shall bear Lord Dray's scorn with equanimity. If he hates me—so much the better. If, as Rebecca suspects, his anger masks a jealous heart, then 'tis better I never know it, for I must marry the Marquis of Rexdale's son and be a dutiful and loving wife.

"Hmmm. You look rather peaked, Halcyon," commented her godmother a few days later. "If I knew no better, I would swear you were pining for a hopeless love!"

A flush rose to Halcyon's cheeks as she took her place beside Lady Henrietta at the breakfast table. She kept her eyes downcast and chose not to reply to her godmother's remarks.

"What ails you, child? Does the air of Bath not agree with you?" Lady Hensham's searching gaze had not missed Halcyon's confusion.

"It is nothing, Godmother. Merely a slight megrim. I think I shall walk in the Gardens today and mayhap that will dispell the gloom I always feel at the onset of a headache."

"I hope you have not forgot that this is the night of Lord Henry's ball for Elizabeth?"

"Oh, I had quite forgot! How remiss of me." Indeed, Halcyon should have remembered that her dearest friend was to be the shining star at the ball this evening. She had been anticipating it all week long. Had not Elizabeth told her that both Lord Medford and Lord Winthrop would be there?

"Have you yet decided what to wear, child?"

"I thought perhaps the silver tulle with the scattered sequins—or is that too elaborate, do you think?"

"I think it will do admirably, my love." Lady Hensham nodded her approval and went on. "There, I do declare that the very thought of the ball has brought the roses back to your cheeks, Halcyon. Have we perhaps been living too quietly? Has there been a dearth of routs, cotillions, and *thés?* Do you

179

long for gaiety and the noise of young people around you instead of an old fuddy-duddy like me?"

"Oh, no indeed, Godmother! I do assure you that your company is all I could wish for, and I find no lack of outings in my life. Indeed, I fancy it is quite the reverse."

"The reverse? How so?"

"I merely mean to say that I have never in my life attended so many functions and gala occasions. Belike the effort is what has caused the peaked look you remarked on, Godmother."

"Hmmm." Another sharp glance from Lady Henrietta convinced Halcyon that she had not deluded that good lady for one minute. If she was to keep her longing for Lord Dray a secret, she was going to have to be very much more careful in future!

"Tell me, Godmother," she changed the subject as she helped herself to toast and preserves, "am I ever like to meet the Marquis of Rexdale's son during my sojourn in Bath? I recall you said it probable, but, to date, he is conspicuous by his very absence, to say the least."

Lady Henrietta chuckled. "Getting curious, are you, girl?"

"You could say that."

"Well, be patient a while longer. I fancy you won't have too long to wait."

"Why? Is he in Bath? Will I perhaps see him this evening?"

"Nay, child, not so fast. He will make an appearance, I am sure, when it suits him. Though when that will be, I am as much in the dark as you are."

"Why all the secrecy?" pouted Halcyon. "I begin to feel somewhat chagrined by this cloak-and-daggar business. Either the Marquis of Rexdale's son intends to marry me or he does not."

"Well, of course he is to marry you! Was that not all arranged long since?"

"So you say . . . But why the long delay?"

Lady Hensham laid down her fork. "Halcyon, my dear, I though that was what you wanted," she stated with some exasperation. "You had every appearance, but a few weeks ago on learning of your arranged betrothal, of a convicted criminal on her way to the gallows. You welcomed the idea of a small respite, a time to become used to the idea that had been sprung upon you so suddenly. And now you are telling me that the delay irks you, that you wish to make the acquaintance of the marquis's son with all speed."

Halcyon sighed. She could not account for her contrary emotions. On the one hand she wished she could delay her marriage to Rexdale's son indefinitely, rub it off the map of her life as though it never need become reality; yet on the other hand she wished she could rush madly, blindly into the arrangement without more thought of Dray and her feelings for him.

"I wish it was all over," she whispered disconsolately.

"Fie, child! That's no attitude for a prospective bride."

"How can I feel excited about someone I have never met, Godmother? How would you feel?"

"I confess I would feel a little . . . intrigued, to say the least, Halcyon. The Marquis of Rexdale's son is a fine figure of a man, much sought after by the ladies. With that knowledge under my cap, I declare I should have my curiosity tickled! Unless someone else were the object of my affections." She flashed a coy glance at Halcyon.

"W-what makes you say that?"

"Only that you have met a bevy of handsome gentlemen these last weeks in Bath. Belike one of them has stolen your heart?"

A deep flush had mounted to Halcyon's face, and she was hard put to conceal her discomfort.

"I-I find the idea sadly lacking in taste," she stammered, "c-considering I am already promised . . ."

She was glad that her godmother then desisted in her inquiries. Halcyon knew that Lady Hensham meant well; if things had not turned out quite the way she had intended, it was not her fault. How was she to have known that Halcyon's unwary heart had been no match for the virile charms of Lord Dray?

As she set off with Rebecca later that day for a stroll in the Sydney Gardens, she did not remark Lord Dray's carriage rattling along the street to stop in front of her godmother's house.

"But why such agitation, Dray?" Lady Hensham gazed with consternation at her friend. "I do declare you have the air of a man pursued by the Bow Street Runners!"

"Pursued by devils, more like," his lordship groaned, running a frantic hand through his hair.

"My dear boy! To what do you refer?"

"To devils of my own making, Lady Henrietta. I am like a man demented—tormented day and night by a vision of loveliness that dances ever farther out of my reach."

"Out of your reach? How so? Explain yourself,

Dray! If the vision of loveliness to which you refer—and I hope it is—is Halcyon, then, as you well know, she is yours for the taking."

"Nay, not so!" He paced back and forth distractedly. He swung around to cast an agonized look in Lady Hensham's direction. "We thought we had managed our affairs so nicely, did we not? 'Let her have her small amusement,' we said. 'Let us play a game of love with her and ensnare her unsuspecting heart in just the way we want.' But it did not work. Our trick rebounded against us."

"Nonsense! Everything is working every bit as smoothly as we intended, I am sure of it. You are overwrought, dear boy—for what reason I can only surmise—and as such you cannot see the truth clearly. Believe me, Dray, our plans will see satisfactory fulfillment. Oh, do stop pacing like a caged tiger. You are like to wear out the carpet." She patted the sofa beside her. "Sit down and let us discuss the matter tranquilly."

"I wish I could have your sanguine outlook, Lady Henrietta," said Dray, complying with her request and placing himself at her side. "I fear, in spite of your reassurances to the contrary, the matter does not go well. How I wish we had stayed far away from this intrigue. I should have made my identity known from the start, you know. Should have grabbed her whilst she was still unaware of all the attraction of the town, before she realized just how many eligible and handsome men were vying for her favors. She was mine—*mine!* If I had played straight, I think I would not have lost her." He groaned and cradled his head in his hands, an unwontedly dejected posture that Lady Hensham had not believed possible for him.

"Come, now, Dray. What arrant nonsense you talk. Halcyon is yours, you know it as surely as I do. Why, since the promise made between your father, the Marquis of Rexdale, and Lucius Glaybourne, there can be no other outcome of this affair."

"I want her not unwillingly, don't you see?" cried Dray. "I thought she would know me and love me before I made myself—my identity—known to her."

"Ah!" Her ladyship tapped him coquettishly on the arm with her fan. "Now I see what is amiss." A beaming smile spread across her features. "You are in love!" She chuckled delightedly. "I never thought to live to see the day. To think that you who have left a trail of broken hearts in your wake now find yourself so sadly smitten! And has Cupid's arrow pierced deep, my lord?" Her amusement died as she saw the expression on Dray's face.

"This is no laughing matter, Lady Henrietta. You are right, of course; I am in love with Halcyon, and no one can be more surprised at that fact than I myself. I have played with love; up till now 'twas but a pleasurable game. But now it is no longer a game, and, as heaven is my witness, it is scarcely pleasurable. It is torture, agony. I would as soon face the rack as go through this. If the lady would but eye me with favor, it would be some mitigation. But she hates me, I tell you, Lady Henrietta; she despises me. Worse, she has eyes only for another!"

"What do you mean?" asked Lady Hensham sharply. "I do declare, boy, love has addled your wits."

"It is the truth." Dray jumped once more to his

feet and resumed his pacing. "Have you not remarked a change in her behavior? Have you been unaware of her many furtive outings of recent weeks?"

"Well, now that you mention it . . ." Lady Hensham's brow creased in worry. "I confess that I have given her a free rein. I had thought to help your cause, dear boy. Foolish woman that I am, I thought she was meeting you. Dear heaven! Tell me that all this is a jest, Dray. Spare me my agony of mind. Do you mean to say that she has . . . Nay! I do not believe it for a moment!"

"Believe it you must."

"I do not believe it! I do not! Halcyon is a sweet, trustworthy child, quite incapable of guile and underhand dealings. On what, pray, do you base your accusations?" She gazed at him imperiously, her head thrown back defiantly as she protected her beloved goddaughter's name.

"I have proof, my lady. Like a jealous husband I have had her watched, and even I myself found her leaving certain lodgings across Pulteney Bridge."

"I . . . can . . . scarce . . ." Lady Hensham reached for her perfumed handkerchief—an ever-present help in trouble—and wafted it agitatedly in front of her nose. "Surely Halcyon would . . . not act so."

"It is our fault, ma'am; on our heads must rest the censure, for did we not deliberately place her in a situation where she was encouraged to seek adventure and fall in love?"

"But . . . 'twas for you, Dray."

"Our conniving has gone against us."

"I suppose you know the blackguard who has trifled with her affections?"

Dray nodded. "That is the worst of it; he is no blackguard, but a gentleman, albeit a poor one. The Earl of Winthrop is a firm friend of mine, ma'am."

"Hmmm. A friend indeed!"

"He is not to blame. I have no doubt he is acting in good faith. If only I had told him of the commitment my father had made on my behalf, none of this pother would have arisen. It was indeed foolish to keep the bargain so secret. Had I not been such a rake, I should have willingly imparted the information to the world at large."

"Nay, do not malign yourself, my lord. This Winthrop—he is the one with whom you have kept such close company all these years?"

"The very same. Now there is a turn of events." Lord Dray smiled grimly. "I cannot recall how many ladies have ignored him whilst setting their caps at me. How often I congratulated myself that I could have the pick of them all! And now see how he basks in my lady's favor whilst I am out in the cold. A somewhat ironical justice, is it not, Lady Henrietta?"

Lady Hensham, however, had no time for ruminating on the vagaries of justice. "No wonder the girl has been showing such an unhappy mein. If I had but suspected . . . but enough of that. The question now of paramount importance is: what do we do now? I could send her back to the country to await her prospective bridegroom . . . or you could reveal now your true identity." She noted Dray's emphatic shake of the head. "No?"

"I am in a quandary; I know not what to do. As you say, by rights she is mine for the taking . . . and yet . . . and yet . . . I would have her willingly.

Wrenching her from the man she loves is scarcely an auspicious start to a marriage, Henrietta."

"Then you must try all the harder to win her affections, Dray. Good heavens, man, you are not unattractive," she said with gross understatement. "Use your charms; surely we women are not the only ones who use what nature has given us to advantage."

"Indeed not." Dray had the grace to smile. "But in fact the miserable truth is that whenever I meet her I am dissolved to a trembling schoolboy. With others I can lay on the spurious charm—but with her . . . ah! It is another matter."

"Fie, my lord! I never thought to see you so," remarked Lady Hensham, considering in amazement what a great leveler was love. The handsome Lord Dray had never lacked for the admiration of women, he had been the rage of many a London season. He was no longer a youth, but his maturity only added to his rampant male charm. And yet here he was, brought to heel not by one of the Court coquettes, but by a fresh and artless girl from the country, confessing himself nervous as a tonguetied, callow youth in her presence. "You will not turn her head or charm her heart with nervous stammerings. Make an effort; play a part; forget the importance of your quest and relax."

"You are no doubt right," nodded Dray. "I shall give the attempt two more weeks. To date I have stood back, feeling that I was an ogre to interfere in her choice of companion but, after all, is it not said that 'all is fair in love and war'? From this moment on I shall be the charming suitor, the ardent lover—"

"Nay, do not go overboard," said Lady Hensham, smiling at his enthusiasm.

They were both laughing as Halcyon, returned from her walk with the rosy cheeks of exertion flaming her face, entered the room.

Immediately Dray went over to her. Startled to find him here, she was however quick to regain her cool composure as she reminded herself that she had promised herself to keep him at a distance henceforth. The light she saw in his eyes made her determination waver only momentarily, and she maintained her icy aloofness as he bent low over her hand and professed himself delighted to see her looking so well and charming as ever.

Neither Lord Dray nor Lady Hensham was slow to notice Halcyon's unresponsive attitude, and with a telling glance at her ladyship, Lord Dray made his departure.

"Halcyon, my dear, you were hardly civilized to Lord Dray. I thought you found him an agreeable companion." Lady Hensham remonstrated as soon as Dray had gone.

Halcyon affected complete indifference. "And so he is agreeable, Godmother, but not more so than many another."

"And why, pray, the frosty looks?"

"I have decided that I shall keep all my acquaintances at bay henceforth. After all, am I not already promised to the son of the Marquis of Rexdale? I shall maintain a most circumspect dealing with all gentlemen from this moment on; let my demeanor proclaim to that good gentlemen, who has taken so long to come forward, that it is time to make himself known, for I have tired of my 'freedom'—if, indeed

188

it was ever anything more than an insubstantial mirage—and am now ready to become a dutiful wife."

"Good heavens, child!" Here indeed was news for Lord Dray. Did he suspect for one moment that Halcyon had reached this stage? Had she quarreled with Lord Winthrop? Had she tired of an infatuation born of boredom? What could be the reason for her sudden desire to speed her marriage, a marriage that had appeared worse than a prison hitherto? Then, remembering Lord Dray's plans to try to win Halcyon's affections in the coming two weeks, she said in softer tones, "Very well, my dear. I shall notify the marquis's son. But, in the meantime—a week or two —pray make an effort to give the pleasures of Bath one more try until your prospective groom is able to join us."

Halcyon agreed. Two more weeks was not so very long, after all. Two more weeks in which to gaze her fill at Dray and to dream of things that would all too soon have to be put aside.

CHAPTER FOURTEEN

Elizabeth's ball was a bittersweet occasion. There were a hundred guests; among them were Lord Medford, Lord Winthrop, Lord Dray, and sundry others whom Halcyon had met at Brampton Court. In spite of his being treated as an honored guest in Sir Henry's house, the impression was received that Lord Medford was in fact the host, so prominently did he feature in the preliminary greetings.

Halcyon shuddered as she felt his fleshy, hot hand grasp hers at the entrance to the ballroom. Ugh! It was horrible! Poor, poor Elizabeth!

Glancing around the ballroom, with its bouquets of flowers, the sparkling decorations that had been affixed to the walls, the festoons of pink and mauve chiffon that wafted in the breeze from the open windows, Halcyon had no doubt that all this splendor and grandeur had been paid for by the repulsive Lord Medford. Now Sir Henry was even more beholden to his lordship.

As Lady Hensham and her goddaughter passed among the gathered guests, nodding amiably to this one or pausing to chat with that, Halcyon's eyes roved eagerly around. Was he here? Surely he had been invited.

It was useless to tell herself that Lord Dray meant nothing to her, to chide her heart for beating so erratically the minute she espied that upright, handsome figure, dressed this evening in a russet satin coat and white inexpressibles with a pristine white neckcloth tied in the mathematical. His hair gleamed with the same burnished highlights as his dress, and, meeting hers across the crowded room, his smoldering gray eyes penetrated her protective armor and pierced her to the very soul. Her body trembled; her limbs would scarcely hold her erect, so devastated was she by that arrogant, compelling gaze.

"Halcyon, my love, you are quite pallid. Do you feel unwell?"

"I shall be all right, Godmother; it is merely the sudden heat brought on by the crush of so many people."

Lady Hensham took her arm. "Precisely my own sentiments, my dear. Let us direct our steps towards the open windows where, no doubt, the breeze will be a blessing."

The windows were the last place Halcyon wished to approach, for was not Lord Dray standing in that vicinity? But Lady Hensham would brook no argument. She chivvied her charge across the room, feigning to be unaware of her reluctance. Out of the corner of her eye she had seen Dray's fiery glance at Halcyon, and she was enjoying herself immensely. The evening had distinct promise.

No sooner had they reached the windows than Dray joined them. He greeted each of them in turn with grace and charm, and to Halcyon's horror her godmother immediately urged him to take Halcyon out into the air.

"She will not admit it herself, Dray, but she finds the heat oppressive. Why, but a moment ago I thought her like to pass out on me. Go along, I shall be quite happy here, I do assure you, for even now I see Clarissa Cranshaw hastening towards us." So saying, she turned her back on the two, dismissing them with an equanimity that showed that she felt that she, at least, had done her best to further Dray's cause.

Lord Dray offered his arm to Halcyon.

"What do you say, Miss Glaybourne? Shall we partake of the sweetness of the night air? Your godmother is right, I declare, for you are quite atremble." The roguish twist of his mouth indicated his awareness that the tremble might not necessarily have been caused by the stuffy atmosphere.

They strolled arm-in-arm in the balmy dusk. Halcyon found herself quite tonguetied, aware in some way that Lord Dray's recent animosity towards her had diminished to some extent; this evening he showed none of his former scorn and contempt. The reason for this change of heart was not apparent, and, not wishing to break the tenuous thread of this new amity, Halcyon guarded her tongue. It would not do to inquire the why and the wherefore; it was enough that he smiled upon her, pressed her arm engagingly to his side, and talked of mundane things in an undertone that made them somehow seem so much more important. She would enjoy her new-found favour in his eyes, she decided, knowing that it might well be short-lived.

"I trust you do not feel the night air too cool?" asked Dray as he felt a little shiver pass through her.

"N-no, indeed. I-I have been too much indoors these last few days and am thankful for the freshness of the air."

"I had noticed that you and Lady Hensham sally

193

forth less than before. Is there anything amiss? Have you tired so soon of the attractions of our fair city?"

"Indeed not," she declared, without elaborating that a few visits to the lending library had provided her with many hours of quiet enjoyment.

"Or is it, perhaps, that you still pine for the green fields, the wild creatures, the joyfully chorusing birds of Glaybourne Manor? Tell me true, Miss Glaybourne, are you homesick?"

"Yes . . . yes, I am, a little." She thought of her dear papa, saw in front of her eyes his rather shabby figure, sitting now, she could well imagine, in the library where a fire would be blazing in the hearth to dispel the slight chill of the evening. Tears threatened her eyes. Oh, she hoped he was taking care of himself! Ever a daydreamer, absentminded to a degree, he was like to have forgotten to put a tinder to the fire. Oh, she should be there herself to see to his needs. How selfish to be here passing her time in idle enjoyment when he needed her! A flood of regrets and shame washed over her and her face took on a disconsolate droop.

"Why, do not look so dejected, Halcyon. I had not thought my mention of your home would bring the clouds to your face. Is not the countryside here to your liking? We, too, have birds and wildlife and a wide expanse of greenery. Is it not the same? Can you not derive pleasure from it?"

"B-but Papa—dear Papa—is not here."

Lord Dray's eyes softened as he looked at her. "You miss your father? . . . Ah, Dear Halcyon, what a sweet and tender-hearted creature you are. Why did not your father accompany you to Bath? I am sure that Lady Hensham's house is large enough to accommodate many more, let alone just one man."

"Indeed, and I am sure that her invitation must have been extended to him. But he would not come. He could not bear to leave his books, his library, his old wing chair by the fire. How I miss him!" she sighed.

"But you must not allow regretful thoughts of him to cloud your present happiness. After the summer you will return to him, will you not, and pass with him many more happy hours." He was gazing at her searchingly, as if much depended on her answer, and of a sudden she realized that he was gently testing to see if, indeed, she planned to return. Why? What could it matter to him? Then she sucked in her breath as she realized that he was probing to discover whether she had any plans to run off with the Earl of Winthrop. Ah! He still did not trust her. The thought saddened her immeasurably.

"Yes, I shall return," she assured him firmly. Too bad that he was unaware of the commitment she had towards the Marquis of Rexdale's son; then he would understand that, of course, she had to return. "I am not unmindful of my duty," she said.

A puzzled frown creased Dray's brow.

"Your duty? To what duty do you refer? Your duty as a daughter?"

"What else?" She fixed on him a cool look. Did he find it so surprising, then, that she should feel the tie of duty? For a moment she was tempted to tell him of her forthcoming betrothal to Rexdale's son—after all, it was scarcely a secret, although her godmother would seem to desire it so. That would explain everything to Dray. He would then understand why she was unable to cast her cap at any man, either Winthrop or himself, and surely he would think more kindly of her thereafter. But no! If he was of a mind to condemn her, then that revelation would only be misconstrued as yet another reason why he should despise her. She would keep silent. Soon she would be away from here and, like as not, would rarely, if ever, meet Dray again.

She swallowed the lump in her throat, and turned bright eyes on Dray. She could at least enjoy her last few days. "Shall we return to the ballroom, my lord? I thank you for your concern in bringing me to take the fresh air, and confess to feeling much recovered."

The moon had risen above the horizon, a glowing, silvery orb that cast an ethereal light over the scene below. Halcyon's curls were bathed in gossamer light, the moonbeams sparkling like tiny dewdrops on her hair; her eyes, deep and mysterious, were cast in shadow, half-veiled by the long lashes that seemed to barricade her thoughts from the outside world.

Lord Dray drew in his breath sharply. What a vision of loveliness she was! And so totally unaware of her charms. An agonizing pain thrust through his chest. And she was his, his to claim when he wished! He should tell her now of his identity, confess and make a clean breast of it out here in the moonlight, where surely the atmosphere would be on his side. But he did not dare! If only he could be sure that her feelings for Winthrop . . .

He looked at her again and a deep longing rose up from within him. He reached out and touched the glory of her hair, and felt the curls spring to life under his touch. Would she spring to life in just such a way, he wondered, at the caress of his hands? He tried to thrust the insistent thought aside, but it refused to be banished. His hands had a will of their own, his fingers seemed determined to tease his tumultuous senses. After running through her hair and loosing the curls from their confining clasp, his fingers moved downward over the curve of her cheek, briefly brushing over the sweetness of her mouth, and then stealing down to the smooth white column of her throat. He felt her tremor as nameless emotions shivered exquisitely through her slender form; she stared breathlessly up at him, mesmerized by the fierce longing blazing deep in his eyes, and then, compelled by an urgent force that could not be denied, she swayed towards him.

Dray's hands ceased their explorations and circled her shoulders to pull her to him. His lips found hers and joined with hers in a ecstasy of sweetness that penetrated Halcyon's newly erected barriers and demolished all her firm intentions.

She reveled in the emotions his kiss awakened in her; she was lost, powerless to resist. Dray's mouth was the only thing that existed for her in the universe, and she raised her arms almost without conscious thought or volition and twined them around his neck, drawing him yet closer, closer, to taste yet more of that heady nectar.

A sudden movement and voices nearby in the shadows caused them to jump violently apart, more shaken by this brief encounter than either of them cared to admit. Halcyon gazed at Lord Dray in consternation, all her fine resolutions flooding back into her mind to plague her now. Had she not determined to keep Lord Dray at bay? Had she not resolved to be cool and aloof, giving him no opportunity either to charm or to repulse her? So much for her fine intentions. They had been discarded to the wind the moment he had reached out and touched her.

"M-my lord," she stammered as the voices that had interrupted them receded into the distance.

"Nay," he grasped her hand and imprisoned it in his. "Call me Tony. What is this nonsense of 'my lord'? Are we not friends. Can you deny that something between us strives for expression?"

"No . . . No!" she cried in agitation. "It can never be! . . . I—forgive me, my lord. What h-happened but a moment ago bodes well for neither of us. It . . . must . . . never happen again." She gazed sorrowfully at him like a wounded fawn poised ready for flight.

"Do not say that, Halcyon," he pleaded, his face set and white. "We were made for each other . . . Come!" He held out his arms. "Let me hold you again like a frightened bird trembling in my embrace. Let me stroke your hair and whisper words of love. Let me confess that—" He had been about to put an end to the misery between them by confessing the ruse he had played on her, aided and abetted by her godmother, but Halcyon would not listen to him.

Throwing an agonized glance in his direction, she placed her hands over her ears. "Enough, my lord. I have told you that it cannot be! Do not torture both of us by these . . . maunderings. I-I have to tell you that I can never love you as you seem to desire." It was the nearest she could get to disclosing that she was promised to another. Before he could answer her or remonstrate further, she picked up her skirts and ran in the direction of the house, pausing briefly outside the double windows of the ballroom to regain a semblance of control and composure. She slipped unobtrusively inside, her cheeks flaming.

Lady Hensham's brows rose in surprise at the sight of her. "Halcyon, my dear—"

"I shall be back directly ma'am," said Halcyon as she brushed past her godmother on her way to the cloakroom. It was imperative that she have a few moments to herself. Once there, alone, gazing into the mirror, she noted the feverish tinge to her cheeks and the blaze in her eyes that gave her a delirious air. She raised trembling hands to her face.

He loves me! she whispered to herself in wonder; I am quite sure of the fact . . . and yet it merely makes it all the more imperative that I should spurn his friendship. Oh! To think that I allowed him to kiss me in that way! I am lost if I allow a repetition of such an act.

She whirled around as someone else entered the room. It was Elizabeth, whose pinched, white face contrasted sharply with her shining, elaborately styled hair, glittering jewels, and resplendent ball gown.

"Elizabeth!" cried Halcyon, her own troubles swiftly forgotten. "What ever is amiss? You have every appearance of despair in spite of your splendid apparel. What can be the matter? I do declare . . . this should be a time of great delight for you; are you not the toast of the evening and the belle of the ball?"

"Oh, Halcyon!" choked her friend. "It is well said that 'fine feathers do not make a fine bird'! You see before you a sham and an imposter. Here I am," she gestured to herself, "decked out in the finery given to me by the man to whom I am promised. These are his pearls; this ring is his; his money bought the fine material for this gown. It is by his grace that we all reside here in Bath this summer, for I know that Papa is quite penniless and could never have reopened the house without the financial backing of Lord Medford."

"Yes, I know that, Elizabeth," said Halcyon gently. "But his lordship has made a bargain that is obviously the more to his advantage than your father's. He made the bargain more than willingly, I am sure. I fail to understand your present qualms."

"But," whispered Elizabeth, "that is just the point; he is not getting the bargain he thought, for I despise him! I have accepted his gifts, and yet I cannot in return give him my heart. For my heart is given to Winthrop and will forever be his."

"Lord Medford must realize that neither his money nor anyone else's can buy love. As long as you are a dutiful and respectful wife to him, he can have no cause for complaint."

Elizabeth shuddered. "How can I be a respectful and a dutiful wife, Halcyon, when I find the man so totally repulsive? I hate him, I tell you, with all my being! Just the look of him fills me with disgust and loathing! And the thought of marrying him and s-suffering his . . . his . . . embrace . . . quite appalls me!" She choked and burst into a fit of bitter weeping.

"Elizabeth, dear, pray cease this weeping," cried Halcyon, kneeling by her friend in consternation. "It cannot be as bad as you say. You must speak to your father; surely he will not suffer his daughter to marry a man she so despises."

"What choice has he, pray?" Elizabeth raised tear-flooded eyes. "He has borrowed heavily from Lord Medford. Regretful though he may be, he is as trapped as I am."

"Have you spoken to him, then?"

Elizabeth nodded. "I did intimate to him that my forthcoming match was not quite what I most desired."

"And . . . ?"

"He started to tremble and his face took on an ashen hue. He was hoarse, I tell you, Halcyon, hoarse as he muttered, 'Daughter, do not fail me now!' . . . Oh! What shall I do?"

"It would appear that you really have no choice," she told her friend slowly. How she wished that she could have offered more hopeful advice, but that was, of course, impossible. Elizabeth had a duty to perform. If she had had the courage to speak up at the very beginning, before her father had committed himself entirely to the mercies of Lord Medford, there might have existed some hope. But she had kept silent, hiding her despair in an illicit friendship with the Earl of Winthrop, and now it was too late to reverse her fortunes.

In such a predicament am I like to find myself if I do not take care, Halcyon told herself sternly. I have already given my word to my father, have let it be known that I shall marry the Marquis of Rexdale's son; I shall have to make the best of it. I myself should take the unpalatable advice I give Elizabeth.

"Dry your eyes, Elizabeth. Since there is no help, you must face forward and tread your path gracefully and with courage."

"It is all very well for you, Halcyon," retorted Elizabeth, who was not a trifle peeved by this seeming lack of sympathy on Halcyon's part, "for it is plain as a pikestaff that you are like to obtain your heart's desire. It has not gone unnoticed the way in which you and Lord Dray look at each other. Why—"

"What ever do you mean?" trembled Halcyon. Was her secret already discovered?

"You are indeed more fortunate than I. You can marry the man of your dreams. Lord Dray—"

"Say no more!" interrupted Halcyon, tight-lipped. "Can you really have forgotten so soon that I am promised to the Marquis of Rexdale's son?"

"But, Halcyon—"

"Say no more, for I shall not listen! Can you really think of me so little that you would suspect me of offering dutiful advice to you whilst reserving for myself the right and the pleasure of denying my duty and turning my back on my father's promise? True, I do love Lord Dray." Her voice trembled at this admission. "He is more dear to me than life itself, more dear than all the things in life save one—my honor! Oh, yes, I understand that honor is an outmoded quality in the high society of London's *ton*, but I nevertheless still hold it dear and, much as I love Dray, much as I dread the thought of another man's arms around me, I shall soon return to the confines of Glaybourne Manor to await the coming of my prospective suitor. And, I beseech you, Elizabeth, if you love me, do not ever refer to Lord Dray again."

She would have sallied from the room, but Elizabeth, who had regarded her in stupefaction and a good deal of admiration during this tirade, held out a detaining arm.

"Pray forgive me, Halcyon; I spoke out of turn. What a good, kind, dear person you are, to be sure. I should have known that you would never give me advice you could not take yourself. Am I forgiven?"

"Of course!" Tearful smiles were exchanged as the two friends embraced. "Now, come, let us return with all speed to the ballroom, for I fear that our lengthy absence will have been noted."

The ball was in full swing. As soon as they returned, both Halcyon and Elizabeth were claimed for dances and whirled onto the floor. Lord Medford led Elizabeth out for a cotillion and as she danced with the Earl of Brampton, Halcyon cast many glances in their direction. Elizabeth's face had a set, unhappy look, and it was obvious that what Lord Medford had to say to her did not agree with her at all. What ever can they be discussing? wondered Halcyon, noting Elizabeth's remonstrances and Lord Medford's heightened color.

The matter became perfectly clear a short time later. Halcyon was dancing with Lord Dray and wished that the music would never end, when Sir Henry Cecil stepped up on the dais and indicated that he would like to say a few words.

"My dear friends," he began. "May I express my delight at your kind presence here with us this evening as we celebrate a ball for our charming elder daughter, Elizabeth. What you do not know is that it is indeed a double cause for celebration, for I have the pleasure tonight of announcing Elizabeth's forthcoming marriage to my dear friend Lord Medford." He gazed around, smiling expansively as though it was indeed in his eyes wonderful news.

There was a surprised ripple running through the

ballroom, and all eyes fastened on the set, white countenance of Elizabeth. She smiled as charmingly as she was able as Lord Medford took her arm and led her to dance to the music that now swelled from the small orchestra. This was a surprise! Halcyon was sure that Elizabeth had not expected this announcement. No doubt it had been sprung upon her by a father who feared that unless the matter was quickly cemented his unwilling daughter would back out of the commitment. It was too late for regrets now. Elizabeth must bear her lot with fortitude. There would be no more clandestine meetings with Lord Charles. Glancing quickly around, Halcyon perceived the tightly agonized face of the Earl of Winthrop. He was as a man who had felt the ground cut from under him. He gazed in horror at Medford leading Elizabeth out, and his throat worked convulsively. His clenched hand stirred at his side, and for a moment Halcyon thought he might be hiding a pistol. He might just be feeling crazy and desperate enough to use it! Yes, she was sure that he struggled with thoughts of vengeance. It would not do for him to speak out of turn now and reveal everything. He must be silenced at all costs.

With a muttered apology to Dray, Halcyon sped across the room and intercepted Winthrop before he could reach Medford. Her hand on his arm, she quietly constrained him.

"Lord Charles, I beg of you. Do not contemplate foolishness at this point."

Dazed, he looked down at her.

"It was not supposed to be this way . . . We had not bargained for this, Halcyon."

"I know, my lord. But it is done now, and there

is no remedying the fact. Stand back, I beg of you; do not draw attention to yourself now."

"I will kill the blackguard!" he ground out.

"Nay, do not say that!"

"It is true! I cannot face the thought of Elizabeth married to a man like that. I would sooner face death and dishonor myself than allow that to happen."

"Have a care at what you say, my lord!" cried Halcyon, and when Winthrop stared at her in consternation, she continued, "Neither your death nor your dishonor will profit Elizabeth now. If you love her—truly love her—then you will let her go; you will make easy for her the path of thorns she has now to tread." She looked up to see the tormented eyes of Lord Dray upon her, and an idea suddenly came to her. "I beg of you, Lord Charles, do not act rashly now. If you need a friend or wise advice, I counsel you to confess your problems to Lord Dray—I understand he is an esteemed friend of yours—and no doubt he will solve many of your woes and prove a staunch ally in times of stress."

She congratulated herself that if indeed Lord Charles took her advice it would kill two birds with one stone; her own actions would be exonerated and Lord Charles would be prevented from rashness and folly that both he and Elizabeth might later regret.

When she returned to Lord Dray he was stiff and formally polite; clearly he was convinced once more that his earlier suspicions of her had been true after all.

Ah! she sighed, it was well said that the course of true love never did run smooth.

CHAPTER FIFTEEN

"Zounds, man, what ails you? Is there any need to apply the whip to such a barbarous degree?"

Lord Dray regarded his friend the Earl of Winthrop most searchingly. It was unlike him to be accused of bad horsemanship, but today he had driven the gig like a madman.

"What ails you? Can you not tell me?" Dray asked the question, but dreaded its answer. This was a subject that should have been broached by them long since; he had a mind to find out the truth about the relationship that existed between Halcyon and the earl, however painful it proved to be.

It was with that intent that he had called on Charles that morning and, upon nearing his lodging, had discerned the slight figure of Sammy hastily beating a furtive retreat.

Aha! So they were up to their old tricks. He had not been unaware that Sammy carried messages from Lady Hensham's house, sometimes stopping at Elizabeth Cecil's, before making speedily for Lord Drewe's lodging.

Springing from his gig, he hurried towards the portico and collided there with Lord Winthrop.

"Why, Charles! I was this very minute coming to see you."

"You have your carriage here?" asked the earl without preliminaries.

"No, the gig."

"No matter. That will do just as well."

Lord Charles sprang into the driving seat and prepared to make off.

"Hey! Steady on, my friend! Am I to be left standing on the cobbles?"

The Earl of Winthrop had the grace to blush. He had quite forgot himself in his anxiety. Only this morning he had received a note from Elizabeth stating that her heart was broken but that she felt bound to incline towards filial duty rather than the dictates of her purely selfish heart. There were to be no more letters, no more clandestine meetings. No more Elizabeth!

The earl whipped the horse in frenzy, quite forgetting his habitual good nature and kindness to animals.

"I have no objection to your driving my equipage, Charles, in the usual course of events," said Dray, removing the reins from his friend's shaking hands, "but today it would appear that you are scarce yourself. Let me take charge of the gig and leave you time to compose yourself . . . and then mayhap you will tell me what all this is about."

They traveled in silence for some time. Dray directed the gig towards the country, skirting the Sydney Gardens and rolling along by the river Avon for some way before finally stopping at a secluded spot that afforded a magnificent view over the undulating green meadows to the purple hills beyond.

Lord Charles had regained most of his composure by this time. He recalled Halcyon's words at the ball. She had urged him to confide in Dray, to tell him his troubles and seek his advice. Well, certainly no harm could come of it now. It would appear that his affair with Elizabeth was well and truly at an end—barring a miracle, that is—and he could lose nothing and perhaps gain much by the calm, unbiased and unemotional opinion of a trusted friend.

He was surprised by Dray's words.

"I can guess the gist of it, my friend . . . You are in love!" Dray decided that a prod in the right direction was needed.

"Exactly!" Charles turned surprised eyes upon him. "But how did you guess? Ah, I believe Halcyon must have told you."

At the mere mention of her name, a shaft of pain seared through Dray's chest. Here was a proof beyond anything he had hoped for; Charles had as good as admitted the matter. Shaken to the core, he merely nodded, and Lord Winthrop continued, "Yes. I am in love, Dray. Laugh at me, scorn me if you will, but I have finally fallen in love."

This time it was Dray who plied the whip and sent the horse scuttling back along the country road in the direction of town. Suddenly he had lost his appetite for a run in the country.

"What, pray, is onerous about falling in love? Why the long looks? Why the sighs? Does not the lady in question"—for the life of him he could not say her name—"return your affection?" he asked rather hopefully.

"Oh, nothing like that, I do assure you; in fact quite the reverse," babbled Charles, thereby dashing those short-lived hopes. "No, Dray, the lady is quite head over heels in love, echoing my sentiments for her in every way."

"Then I see no problem whatsoever," declared his friend savagely.

"Ah! But you have not heard the whole of it. Although we love each other dearly, we are to be torn apart, for she has been promised to another by her doddering old fool of a father. Can you imagine that, Dray? The barbarity of it! To promise a girl to a man she does not know and then to expect her to turn her back on her very dear love to follow the dictates of duty. I tell you, Dray, the very idea is repulsive."

"Is—is that what she has told you?"

"Yes, indeed. She shivers with revulsion at the very thought of his touch . . . told me so herself."

"And why can you not speak to the father and—er —change his mind?"

"Ah! Money, there's the crunch, Dray. The greedy old beggar wants to marry her off to a man with money. In my impecunious state I scarcely qualify for footman in his eyes."

"I see." Dray was silent for a long time after that. Could it really be that Charles was not aware that he, Lord Anthony Dray, was the other suitor, the one to whom Halcyon was promised? Had Halcyon never mentioned that the suitor chosen for her by her father was the son of the Marquis of Rexdale?

Here indeed was an ironical situation! How was he best to advise his friend, when any good advice would surely put his own nose out of joint?

"You must follow the dictates of your conscience," he told him evasively. "No man can do more than that."

"That's just what I say myself," approved the earl. "My conscience will not allow me to see the girl sacrifice her happiness. I shall do my utmost to make her see reason. Though I must say it is like to be a difficult task, for she is bent on doing her duty . . . Foolish child! How noble, how wonderful she is, Dray! I am sure you would love her if you but knew her as well as I do."

Dray smiled to himself with grim humor. Well-spoken words, with more than a ring of truth in them.

"Do you think to persuade her, then?"

"I mean to try. I shall convince her that we should elope. That is my plan, Dray, and I mean to put it into action at the very earliest . . . Say, Dray, have a care! Now it is you who whips the horseflesh!"

Sammy raced along the street, his heart thudding painfully in his chest. Although he was exhausted long before reaching the house occupied by Lady Hensham on the Crescent, he knew that time was of the essence and to delay might mean his mother's life.

He ran up Milsom Street, neatly dodging the carriages, heedless of the fact that he was very nearly crushed by one or two of them, only the adroit horsemanship of the drivers saving him. He turned into the Circus; he dared not slacken his pace. How terrible his mother had looked! He was sure that something very serious was amiss, for although she had tried to smile and assure him to the contrary, her face was deathly white, beaded with perspiration, and her lips had had a bluish tinge.

At last Sammy came to the Crescent. Not waiting to knock on the servants' door this time, he burst in, coughing and rasping after his extended exertion.

"Rebecca!" he gasped hoarsely to a surprised scullery maid who had come to see what all the commotion was about. "Tell Rebecca . . . I must see . . . her!"

A wide-eyed, alarmed Rebecca was speedily brought forth.

"Why, what is the matter, Sammy?" she cried, and then, ushering him into a corner where no one could hear their words, she asked, "Is it Miss Elizabeth? Has there been some trouble?"

"Oh, no, miss," gasped Sammy, now beginning to regain his speech. "It's me mum! Oh, come quick, please, for I fear she's adying!"

Halcyon, coming in search of Rebecca with a note for Elizabeth, heard these last words.

"Make haste," she cried. "Fetch my cloak, and your own, and together we shall see what can be done for the good lady. Sammy, you speed back to her and we shall follow with all due haste."

Nodding his gratitude, Sammy was off. He had known that dear Miss Halcyon would not fail him in a time of trouble!

When Halcyon and Rebecca arrived at the dilapidated hovel near the city walls, Sammy was anxiously sitting by his mother's side. His mother was stretched out on a bundle of straw on the floor, covered by a tattered blanket. Her eyes stared glassily to the ceiling and her breathing came in shuddering gasps. Sammy was manfully trying to wipe the sweat off her forehead with a dirty rag; in the corner of the room huddled his small brothers and sisters, warily watching the proceedings.

He turned as Halcyon and Rebecca entered.

"Thank God you've come! She ain't doing too well

at all, as you can see for yerselves. Now, come on," he chided his brothers and sisters, "Stop your gawping! Outside and play! Aven't I already told you that mum's feeling poorly today?"

"Is she goin' to die?" asked one little ragamuffin, too young perhaps to understand the implications of such a happening, whilst another one, a little girl, began to sob.

"I-I don't want for 'er to die, Sammy," she whimpered. "D-do s-somefink!"

"Naw, she ain't about to die. I tell yer, she's just a-weary and a-tired. These ladies 'ere will help, never fear; now off to play with yer!"

They quickly scattered.

As Sammy stood up to make room for Rebecca at his mother's side, he swayed and fell against the wall.

"Careful, Sammy; are you all right?" asked Halcyon, noting his poor color and the flash of pain that had crossed his face.

"It-it's nothing, miss. I just get these headaches, see."

"But . . . you assured me that they were less frequent now."

"And so they was, until I fell down this morning as I was racing to the Crescent for your help. Oh, miss, me 'ead 'asn't stopped aching since then."

"Sit down," she commanded. "It looks as if we have two people in desperate straits," she called to Rebecca, who was bending over Sammy's mother. "How is she?"

"She ain't good," was Rebecca's verdict. "She's goin' to need her strength with the baby coming and all—and she just ain't got any, miss. No, I don't like the looks of 'er at all."

"Can you do anything for her?" asked Halcyon, anxiously approaching the bed. "How soon before the baby comes?" How helpless she felt as she gazed at the moaning woman. Experience of birthing babies was not in her very limited repertoire, and she was quite at a loss as to what to do.

"Don't worry, miss." Rebecca glanced at her mistress and saw her fear and uncertainty. "It won't be the first little'un I've helped into this world, though I do think that not everything is right this time."

After a few more minutes, Rebecca was sure.

"It's not right; it should have made an appearance by now. Seems like something is 'olding it up."

"What shall I do? Can I help?" Halcyon hovered anxiously on the sidelines, not knowing whether to aid Rebecca or to concentrate her attentions on Sammy, whose face was crumpled in agony.

"I think you'd better send fer the doctor, miss, for I don't like the way things is going here. Sammy could run for help, maybe." She gazed uncertainly at Halcyon. "Me mum's had countless little 'uns and never a mite of trouble, but . . . 'Ere! Wot's wrong with *'im?*" For the first time she noticed that another crisis was taking place in the room. "Wot is it, love?"

"It-it's me 'ead . . . Hurts something . . . terrible!"

"Now, now then. Just lie still." Her alarmed eyes met Halcyon's. "'Ere's a right pickle for us! I shall go for 'elp, miss. You'll just 'ave to stay here and take care of the pair of em . . . Think you can manage?"

"Oh! . . . No . . . I—oh, how inadequate I feel, Rebecca! I know nothing of the birth of babies, although I am more than willing to learn—but it scarcely seems the right time to do it now with a sick woman depending on the skill of my ministrations.

No, I shall have to go for help and you must stay here and do whatever you can."

Rebecca did not like to see her mistress wandering alone in this rough neighborhood, but what else was to be done? Although she had offered to go herself, she well knew that Halcyon would be very little help to Sammy's mother.

"Yes, you go, miss. But do 'ave a care!"

With one last look at the groaning woman, and another at Sammy, who appeared to have lapsed into unconsciousness, she hurried out of the house. What a predicament this was—not one invalid, but two! Sammy's sickness could not have come at a worse time. Halcyon berated herself for not making sure that Sammy's head was completely better. No doubt he had been ignoring the fleeting pains in his head, and the fall today had aggravated an already existing condition. She blamed herself; it had been her responsibility to see that the boy was well, for was he not now in her employ? And was it not her fault in the first place that had caused the injury to his head?

Her thoughts completely on these matters as she hurried along, Halcyon did not see the interested and ominous glances cast at her by many a lingering beggar in the dirty streets through which she traveled. She was intent only on reaching the house of the doctor who had visited Sammy's mother a few weeks ago.

One slovenly creature dressed in rags scrambled to his feet as she passed. His face was covered in sores and his bony hands made to clutch at her. Feeling something touch her, Halcyon turned and beheld his leering, evil face close to hers. With a shriek of terror she took to her heels as though demons pursued her.

She dared not pause to look back. Was he following her?

She heard footsteps close behind her own, pounding feet that echoed the stamp of her own. Fast! Fast! She told herself. Oh! He must not catch her! But he was gaining on her; surely the sound of his feet was closer; surely she could hear his gusting breath.

Suddenly two hands reached out and grabbed her. Horror, terror and revulsion swept over her. She fought like a wildcat trying to escape the binding arms.

"Unhand me you rogue! Let me go, I say!"

She kicked out and heard an exclamation of pain as her foot connected with some part of the villain's anatomy.

"Zounds, Halcyon, this is a poor way to repay your deliverer!" The voice of Lord Dray came to her astonished ears.

Once her struggles had ceased, she was released and immediately she turned to face him. His expression was stern and uncompromising as he returned her searching look.

"Nay, do not regard me so hostilely, Miss Glaybourne, for had I not come to your rescue you might be in a far worse situation now."

"Then . . . I thank you, my lord."

"As well you might. Have you no sense of propriety, to be walking abroad in a district such as this? If you have no thought of your reputation, at least you could consider your safety."

"My reputation is perfectly whole, my lord, thanks to me—and now my safety also, thanks to you," she replied stiffly.

"Huh! I can scarce believe that; I recall only too

well an occasion in Lord Brampton's garden when it was proved just how futile were your attempts to guard your reputation." His eyes blazed at her, partly in anger and partly in remembrance of those few brief moments when his lips had claimed hers in an unwilling kiss.

Oh! The man was utterly insufferable. It seemed he could think no good of her.

"Where have you been this time? A clandestine meeting with a secret admirer? A rendezvous with Winthrop?" His lips curled disdainfully and his glance raked her disheveled form from head to toe. "And why are you running? Did he make overtures you found distasteful? Did your courage fail you at the last moment?" He reached out and shook her savagely, completely forgetting that no gentleman treats a lady so.

"N-no! You have it all wrong!" Trust him to think that she had been secretly meeting with Lord Charles! "It is n-not that at all! Oh!" Suddenly she remembered the purpose of her excursion. She had quite forgot the matter in her headlong flight. "Help me, Dray," she implored him. "Help me!" A sob caught in her throat and immediately her companion was contrite.

"Help you?"

"I—we need speedy aid. Even now as the minutes are flying the welfare of two—no, three—people hangs in the balance."

"Calm yourself! If this is a serious matter—and it certainly appears so—you had better explain the matter quickly and coherently, Halcyon." He drew her to the side of the street. "Now, who is in danger? And how?"

217

"Sammy's mother . . . and Sammy himself, too . . . Oh, if I had but known his head was bothering him."

"Sammy is the boy who runs errands for you?"

"Yes!" Round eyes widened. "H-how did you know?"

"Never mind. Time enough later for explanations. Of paramount importance now is the boy . . . and his mother, you say?"

"Yes. She is in dire need of a doctor. Sammy came to ask our help."

"Our?"

"Yes, Rebecca's and mine. Thank the good Lord that Rebecca knew what to do, for I confess that I should have been quite inadequate in the situation. She saw immediately that a doctor was needed and Sammy should have been sent to bring one, but he took ill, too. It is all such a muddle, is it not?"

As they had been talking, Lord Dray had guided her footsteps along the road to where a gig awaited.

"Let me help you up, Halcyon. We shall make haste for a doctor. Never fear, we shall do our best to save these two—how three?—people."

Of course Halcyon had found it quite impossible to mention the delicate matter of the baby that was even now perhaps thrusting its way into an unfriendly world. She left Lord Dray to make of the matter what he pleased and, by the small, kind smile on his face, she decided that he must have guessed.

The doctor was speedily dispatched to Sammy's house.

"We must follow," commanded Halcyon, but Lord Dray would not hear of it.

"I think not. I shall return you to your godmother

218

and shall then see what is to be done. Rest assured that if there is help needed it shall be given."

She would have to be content with that for the moment, Halcyon reflected as she stood by the window of the salon and watched his gig rattling over the cobbles back towards town.

It was fortunate that Lady Hensham was not at home, for Halcyon did not know what explanations she could have made. She was unwilling to be underhand with her godmother, but how would she be able to explain her acquaintance with Sammy without implicating Elizabeth? She had better be ready with some semblance of the truth, for surely Lord Dray would divulge much of the matter when he returned.

Rebecca described the most recent events when she returned to the house later that day. "Oh, my, miss, is that a powerful gentleman of yours. I do declare that I never saw matters so speedily and competently taken care of. It was in no time at all, miss, that Lord Dray had the doctor there and was himself a pillar of strength. Declared that no effort or expense was to be spared, he did, and straightaway Sam's mother was administered to like the King 'imself.''

"Will she be all right?"

"Well, miss, that remains to be seen, for she was proper sick, you see."

"And the baby?"

"Right as rain; a boy, miss!"

"Ah, good . . . But who will care for the children? Has Sammy been taken care of?"

"Now, don't fret. Lord Dray took Sammy off to a cousin of his; said the lady would be more than happy to nurse 'im back to good health. And as for the young 'uns—'is lordship came to the rescue again. He made such lavish arrangements for them that like as not the poor bairns is bound to think they is in 'eaven! Yes, indeed, miss, a powerful man is 'is lordship!"

CHAPTER SIXTEEN

Lord Dray was waiting for her when she returned the next morning from her habitual stroll in the Gardens. She was pleased to see him and came straight into the salon to greet him.

"I cannot sufficiently express my thanks for your timely help yesterday, Lord Dray. Without you the story might have had a very different ending. Tell me, have you news of Sammy and his mother?"

"They are both on the road to recovery, I am happy to say. His mother will speedily be fully recovered, for her body will mend as fast as her indomitable mind. For Sammy the recovery may be slower."

"How so? Is he very ill?"

"The doctor professed himself somewhat puzzled by his condition. We can only wait and hope that time will heal the damage done to his head either by his recent fall or in his earlier escapade."

"Oh dear, and it was my fault, too."

"How can you say that? I was not aware that any blame was to be apportioned to you. Sammy, certainly, does not blame you for his condition."

"Nevertheless, it was whilst trying to prevent the theft of my reticule that he sustained that first injury."

"I remember the incident." He remembered also the way he had carried her to his lodging when she had fainted, and his eyes burned at the memory.

"I—" He seemed ill at ease. "It seems I owe you yet another apology, Halcyon," he said quietly. "Once again I mistrusted your actions and believed that you were engaged in underhand dealings when all the time you were—like a very angel from heaven—helping the needy."

"You need offer no apologies, Lord Dray. I will not deny that your lack of trust sorely grieves me, but I can only be relieved that at last you have seen the truth. Now surely you will believe me when I say that, just as I was innocent in this matter, so was I always innocent. Do you believe that now?"

How could he fail to believe it? Had she not vindicated herself of all his former suspicions with this latest event? She waited, trembling, for his reassurance.

She waited in vain. Lord Dray could not say the words she wanted so badly to hear. He gazed at her in torment, not knowing how to tell her. He could not believe in her innocence, since Winthrop had admitted only a day or two ago that he was planning to persuade her to elope with him. And to think that she could look so innocent, knowing all the while that, in love with Winthrop, she planned to go against her father's wishes for her to marry Rexdale's son! The knowledge tormented him. How he wanted to believe otherwise! But he could not. Had not the evidence of his own eyes proved that she had many times sent poor Sammy to Lord Charles's lodgings? Had he not found Halcyon's pendant at the pawnbroker's?

How could a woman who looked so fair act so false? That was the burning question in his mind. He should confront her with his knowledge. He should tell her of his identity—how that would shock her!—and insist that she cease immediately this foolish affair with his friend.

But even as the thought raced through his head, he knew he could not do this. He could not confront her. If she wished to elope with Winthrop, then she must do it. It was her decision to make, and she must be allowed to make it without his interference. Was not that the whole purpose of this foolish masquerade? He had resolved from the start that Halcyon should be given the opportunity to fall in love; he disliked arranged marriages as much as she did. But the intention had been that she should fall in love with him! He had planned to bedazzle and bemuse her and then divulge that he was the Marquis of Rexdale's son and her prospective husband. He had imagined that she would be overjoyed. He had only met her once in the woods near Glaybourne Manor, but even then, before he realized her identity, he had been attracted to her. She had been fresh as a breath of country air, and he had found his senses quite captivated.

When Lady Hensham had proposed her idea, he had accepted it with alacrity. And as time went on he had realized that the gentle, lively girl from the country, so devoid of the guile and pasteboard gilt of the town, held him totally bewitched. And now he had to stand by and watch her throw her heart to another. If she loved the Earl of Winthrop, who was he to stand in her way? He wanted her happiness above all else.

She was waiting now for him to speak, a puzzled frown on her face; she could not understand his silence. Why would he not acknowledge that he now held her to be blameless of all the accusations he had hurled at her? Dimly she realized that, in spite of all she had done, she had failed to make him think well of her, had failed to dispel the lingering culpability that he saw in her.

Her shoulders sagged and the luster went out of her eyes. "It seems, my lord, that you cannot think well of me, whatever I do." She felt utterly faint-hearted and weary. This constant seesaw of emotions could not be endured. "I can do no more to convince you. Mayhap when the doctor sends his bill for his services, you will let me know and I shall find some means of paying it—as I did last time." She swung away from him and prepared to leave the room.

"Wait!" he urged. He was utterly amazed. "As you did last time? You have used his services before?"

"Yes," she nodded. "Sammy's mother was very sick a few weeks ago and I urged him to visit her."

"And you paid him?"

"He would scarcely go else." She smiled in a wintry way.

"How, may I ask, did you manage to pay him? Did you enlist the aid of your godmother?"

"No, indeed! I could not ask her for more than she has already so unselfishly given. I sold my pendant—the ruby one, do you not recall?"

"Of course I do." He bit his lip.

"Why did you question me and seek to trap me? I declare this is quite insufferable! Are you so lacking in trust?" Tears sparkled in her eyes as she confronted him.

"I thought—"

"You thought I had pawned them to pay the Earl

of Winthrop for—for . . . Oh! I will not tolerate this, my lord!" She swung on her heel and rushed from the room.

No, she would not stay a moment longer in his presence! To think that he would believe her capable of paying a man for his favors. He had no reason, no proof, for thinking so. He did her a gross injustice, and he was not the man she had thought him to be. She had thought him kind, compassionate, honorable, and trusting. Instead he was arrogant, harsh, suspicious, and small-minded.

I do not love him! she told herself. I do not! I would not love him if he were the last man on earth. I care even less for him than he cares for me.

Then why did she feel so destitute?

Halcyon had decided to return to her father's house. There seemed little but heartache to be gained by staying in Bath. Her godmother had settled nicely into a pleasurable life here; she had all her old acquaintances flocking around her, and most of her time was taken up with them. She will not be lonely if I leave, thought Halcyon; I may have a clear conscience about that. And what else is there to keep me here? Elizabeth will soon be married, and I doubt not that Lord Medford will carry her off to wilt in his country estate. No, there is nothing else to keep me.

But just as it seemed she was not needed by anyone, there was an unexpected turn of events.

One morning a letter was carried to the servants' door by a stranger. It was a note from Elizabeth.

"I must see you," she wrote in an unsteady hand that clearly betrayed her unease. "I can no longer bear to be apart from Charles. Meet me in the Abbey at one. Do not fail me."

She is going to do something foolish, I know it! Halcyon's anxiety was such that she could hardly get through the morning.

Elizabeth was waiting for her inside the Abbey in the spot least frequented by visitors.

"I am so relieved that you have come," she gasped. I am convinced our secret is out!"

"Sit down. Be calm, Elizabeth. Now do tell me slowly—and coherently if you please—just what all this is about." It was apparent that her friend was on the verge of hysteria. She pressed her into a seat in the shadows and patiently waited for her to gather her wits together.

"I simply . . . cannot marry . . . that dreadful man!"

"I supposed as much. But what do you propose to do about it?"

"I . . . Charles and I have discussed it thoroughly . . . we will elope."

Halcyon gasped. "A dangerous proposition! How do you plan to do that, since your movements are watched so closely?"

"That is where you come into the picture, Halcyon dear. Oh, you will help us, Halcyon? Please say that you will! It will be for the last time, I promise you!"

Such bold words! Halcyon doubted whether it would be as simple as that. "How can I help?"

"You can invite me to stay with you tomorrow night—no doubt an adequate excuse can be concocted."

"How will that help you?"

"Don't you see? I shall not be missed if there is a

226

perfectly reasonable excuse for my being away from home. I shall not be watched in your house. Charles will come for me in the middle of the night, and we can escape and be far away before anyone realizes what has happened."

Halcyon stared at her friend for some minutes. What a difficult position she was being forced into by these two ardent lovers! To help them in this way would incriminate her in the eyes of all concerned, for it would be useless to protest that she knew nothing of the planned escape. She sighed. It had never even occurred to Elizabeth that whilst she would be scores of miles away with her beau, Halcyon would be up to her neck in hot water. However, the memory of Lord Medford quickly chased away all her objections, and she agreed to do what she could to help her friend.

"I'm not pretending that I like or agree with what you are doing, mind you," she said sternly, "But I can fully appreciate why you have come to this drastic act."

They eventually agreed upon a plan. Elizabeth was to arrive at the house the following evening with some samples of material to show Halcyon. They would examine them upstairs in Halcyon's room, pretending to be discussing excitedly the plans for Elizabeth's wedding to Lord Medford. On the way downstairs, Elizabeth would contrive to slip and injure her ankle. "Be careful you do not really hurt it," advised Halcyon, "or we shall be in a pickle!" Owing to the lateness of the hour, and the slight injury, Elizabeth would be pressed to stay overnight at the Crescent.

"Splendid," beamed Elizabeth. "Nobody will suspect."

"I hope you are right," muttered Halcyon with far less conviction.

With such well-laid plans, what could possibly go wrong? Elizabeth was convinced of the success of her elopement, and was vivacious and happy as Halcyon had never seen her.

"Remember, you are not out of difficulties yet," she warned her friend. "Do not presume success until it is yours."

"I have no doubt that all will be well, Halcyon. See how easily I convinced Lady Hensham, my dear aunt, that I had mildly sprained my ankle! Did you not truly admire that fine piece of acting as I tripped down the stairs?"

"It was well done. And it was my godmother herself who suggested that you were better to rest here for the night."

"How simply everything fell into place! That is what comes of scheming the matter so well. Now all we have to do is to make sure that we do not fall asleep and miss Charles when he comes for me."

"Did he say when he would come?"

"As soon as the streets are deserted. It would not do to be seen by a curious passer-by and so spoil everything."

"I hope he will not ride the carriage to the door?"

"No. That is why I must keep a sharp lookout. He will stop over there," she pointed through the window, "by that far streetlight. I shall creep noiselessly downstairs and out the front door. Oh, to think that very soon now we shall be married! Halcyon, is that a carriage I hear?" She ran back to the windows.

"Rest easy, Elizabeth. It is much too early yet. There are still too many people on the streets for you to make good your escape. Be patient now. If you would like to sleep, I can keep watch for a while," she offered.

"No, no! I am much too excited for sleep. Oh, time passes so slowly. What is keeping him?"

When a carriage finally drew into the Crescent and came to a standstill in the shadows across the street, Halcyon and Elizabeth slipped down the stairs as quietly as they could.

Halcyon unlocked the big door and allowed her friend to pass through.

"You're sure that is the earl?" she whispered.

"Certain. Yes, that is his equipage." They hastily embraced. "Goodbye, Halcyon. I can never thank you enough."

"You don't have to. Go quickly now whilst the street is deserted."

"I will write to you when . . ."

"Yes, yes . . . quickly!"

Halcyon was worried. She did not like the unnatural silence of the night. The deserted Crescent seemed altogether too still.

She watched Elizabeth hasten across the cobbles, her feet making not the slightest sound. Dressed in dark clothes, she was scarcely distinguishable from the shadows of the iron railings and the torch extinguishers at the doorway of each house.

She came to the carriage and a dark form helped her inside. The moon came out from behind a cloud. Suddenly everything seemed to happen at once. Just as the carriage was about to rumble away, there was the sound of a voice raised in anger; from the shadows further down the street several dark figures emerged. They ran towards the carriage. There were several gunshots. The horses, startled, reared and bucked and took off blindly, with the carriage careening and swaying madly behind. At that very moment another carriage appeared from the opposite direction; the two equipages met head-on, collided with a sickening crash that sliced through the air like an explosion. One carriage twisted onto its side, the other one rose several feet into the air and turned a somersault before landing.

There were flying figures, cries of anguish, shouts for help, and a flurry of figures in the street.

Halcyon found her own feet carrying her across the cobbles with frantic haste. She heard a strident voice:

"Egad, sir, come out and show yourself! Did you think to carry her off without a fight? Stand forth, sir!"

Portly Lord Medford cut a ridiculous figure as he stood on the corner of the street whilst other, more practical figures rushed to aid the occupants of the carriages.

A tall, familiar figure was frantically pulling away torn pieces of the carriage. Halcyon wondered briefly how Dray had come upon the scene. She heard him cursing and muttering as he sorted through the rubble, and her surprised ears could hardly believe what he was saying.

"My God, Halcyon!" he cried. "Are you conscious? Answer me, answer me!" He lifted the inert body of Elizabeth from the wreckage and tenderly carried it to the verge of the road. "Get a doctor, quick, someone," he cried hoarsely as he bent to examine the girl. "Hal—Elizabeth? . . . What is this?"

"I am a doctor. Stand back," commanded a figure stepping from the crowd that had gathered.

Lord Dray did so as one who is in a dream. He had expected to find Halcyon, instead of which . . . He raised puzzled eyes to search the crowd. All at once his gaze alighted on Halcyon as she stood there trembling, her face pale as death.

"Halcyon!"

He was like a man who has seen the vision of a promised land swim before his vision. He took two great strides forward, clasped her in his arms, and half-urged, half-dragged her back to her godmother's house.

"B-but Elizabeth and Lord Winthrop," stammered Halcyon, looking back over her shoulder at the wretched scene.

"They are being attended to. Presently I shall return to see what is to be done. But come now. I want to see you safely inside. My God! Halcyon, do you know what I went through tonight? I thought it was you in there!" His hands were torn and bleeding from his efforts to free the injured pair from the broken coach, but he would not allow Halcyon to have them bathed. "I must return to the street," he said. "Thank God you are safe!"

By this time half the household was awake. Lady Hensham appeared sleepily, and Rebecca was despatched to the kitchens to provide a hot toddy to settle Halcyon's nerves, for by now she was stuttering and trembling and unable to give a coherent account of what had happened. The butler was sent out into the street to ascertain the extent of the catastrophe, returning very soon with a complete account of all that had taken place, and the news that miraculously neither Elizabeth nor Lord Winthrop was badly hurt.

"Although it appears that Lord Winthrop has been challenged to a duel by Lord Medford."

Lady Hensham looked grim. "I knew trouble would come of my brother's determination to marry the girl off to that man!" she said as Halcyon slid into a faint.

CHAPTER SEVENTEEN

In spite of the shock she had received, Halcyon slept soundly for the rest of that night and halfway through the next morning. When she awoke to see the sunlight streaming in through her windows and casting dancing shadows on the floor of her room, it seemed as if this were a day just like any other and nothing untoward or unusual had happened in the night. Then her thoughts flew to Elizabeth.

Poor, dear friend! Her heart thumped in sympathy for her. They had said that she was not badly hurt, merely scratched and shaken, the same as Lord Charles. For that at least they should all be thankful; it was in itself a miracle, for it seemed impossible to have survived such a crash.

Halcyon would never forget the thundering impact of those two carriages. It would be forever emblazoned on her memory. Poor Elizabeth and Charles! They had only wanted happiness in each other's arms, but they had been caught in the act and now surely would be kept apart forever.

One thing puzzled and teased Halcyon's brain. How had Lord Medford known what was going on? They had taken such great pains to meet only in secret, and always with Halcyon as decoy.

The more she thought about it, the more she realized that she was not surprised by the turn of events. All along she had had a feeling that all was not well.

She had suspected that only bad could come of the deceptions they had practiced. But she had so wanted for Elizabeth to find her happiness. Well, it just was not to be. . . .

Two certainties had come out of the previous evening's events. It just would not do to kick against the dictates of one's duty. Halcyon felt certain of that. Yes, she had been right to decide to return to her father's house, where she would be out of the way of temptation. If it had not been for Elizabeth and her mad scheme, she would have already left. And, as soon as the business of the duel was settled, she would be free to take her leave. She must turn her back on Dray, although when she thought back to the previous evening and saw again in her mind his devastated face when he had thought her to be one of the occupants of the shattered carriage, her body trembled.

She must be strong! One's own happiness seemed a small sacrifice weighed against the confusion and bitterness and disgrace that snatching one's own happiness imposed on others.

Of another thing she was now certain. It concerned Lord Dray. He loves me! He truly loves me! I can no longer doubt that. And all the ignominious accusations he has cast at me have only been because he so loved me and thought that I was planning an elopement with the Earl of Winthrop. What in heaven's name made him think that? I told him the contrary often enough. But still he did not believe me. How pained, how desperate he must have been! I can forgive him his unjust charges in the circumstances. I wonder, though, how he came to know of the planned elopement? Both he and Lord Medford seem to have been very much in the know. I am sure that I did not at any time allow anyone to suspect the truth. Sammy is sick and did not know of the arrangements, and I am sure that Rebecca would breathe a word to no one.

If only she could have saved Lord Dray from that frightful scene in the Crescent last evening. The sight of his tortured face gazing at Elizabeth's crumpled form, the sound of his hoarse cries had convinced her that he was a man truly, totally in love. And with her! A warmth rose within her and a feeling of complete contentedness settled over her. This is the important thing, the thing I must remember. He loves me! And although I shall never be able to turn my back on my duty as Elizabeth did, that thought will always be a comfort to me.

It is good that I shall not see much more of him. That was Elizabeth's mistake. She spent too much time with the earl and became too dependent on his company, until finally she could not do without him, could not conceive of a life that did not include him. I must be careful. I must leave as soon as Elizabeth is settled. Then I shall return to Glaybourne Manor and wait there in seclusion until such a time as the Marquis of Rexdale's son wishes to make me his wife.

She summoned Rebecca and dressed slowly, taking care and time over her toilet. Today she would tell Lady Hensham of her plans to return to Solchester.

She was barely ready when her godmother came into her room. She made no allusion to the events of the night before. "Halcyon, Lord Dray is waiting for you in the salon. He says that he simply must speak with you."

Her heart rose into her throat. He was here! How she longed to rush down the stairs and fling herself into his arms! All the more reason to be firm, she told herself, taking her time before she finally descended the long staircase and entered the salon.

He was standing by the window. He turned as she entered and then came quickly towards her, holding out both of his hands in the most natural way, as though completely sure of a new understanding between them.

It was her undoing. She could not deny it. She accepted his hands in hers and stood returning his smile. Their glances held, caressing each other and speaking volumes without words.

"My dearest," said Lord Dray at last. "You know, you cannot doubt now, that I love you."

She could only nod; the happiness in her heart overflowed. She was too full for words.

"And you love me, too." He was sure of it. "I saw it last evening in your eyes. I knew then, as I looked deep into your eyes and read their joyous message, that there was no one else. There isn't, is there? Let me hear it from your own lips."

"Of course there is nobody else. And certainly not the Earl of Winthrop."

"What a fool I was! A blind fool!"

"I tried many times to tell you that there was nothing between the earl and myself. But you refused to listen."

"Because I was jealous. But why did you tell me that there was someone else? That was a lie, surely?"

"Not quite." Her gaze darkened, and she gently

tried to withdraw her hands. The time had come to reveal all and explain to Dray why she never could be his . . . if, indeed, that was what he wanted. She must forestall him before he spoke his suit. "You see, in a sense, there is someone else. Someone who is between us and always will be. Because of him, you and I shall never be able to . . . to . . ."

"What nonsense is this?"

"I should have told you previously. B-but my godmother assured me that the omission was of minimal importance. It appears that my father made a promise to the Marquis of Rexdale that I should marry his son when I reached the age of seventeen. I knew nothing of this promise. It was a surprise to me just recently."

"And you intend to abide by that arrangement? This marquis's son—he is the one who keeps us apart? There is no one else?" She could not understand why he appeared so relieved.

"Of course I mean to abide by the promise! Would you have me do anything else? Would you have me throw my father's wishes—not to mention his honor —to the winds?"

"In spite of us—of what we feel for each other?"

"In spite of that." She was adamant.

"How can you say that?" He left her side and turned away from her so that she could not see his face. He paced up and down the room several times and then he stopped as though coming to a sudden decision. "In any case, it doesn't matter. I have something to tell you, Halcyon."

She interrupted him.

"What do you mean, 'It doesn't matter'?"

237

"I have something to tell you, my darling . . . something that will make you change your mind."

Halcyon could hardly believe what she was hearing. Was Dray really trying to persuade her to go against the dictates of her conscience? "If it is something that will make me turn away from the path of my duty, I do not wish to hear it, my lord."

"But—"

"No, my lord!" She placed her hands over her ears. "Not another word. I do not wish to hear your remonstrances, your impassioned pleas, for they would all too surely weaken my resolve."

"You accepted—nay, organized and abetted—Elizabeth's rebellion. Yet you will not do the same for yourself?"

"Elizabeth chose her path; I merely helped to clear the way for her . . . and a sorry job we made of it, too. Oh, Dray! What will happen now? Is it true that there is to be a duel? Cannot the matter be settled without such harsh measures?"

Dray regarded her sorrowfully and yet with a sort of admiration. She had time for compassionate thoughts of her friend even in her own sorrow. "You know there is no other way out. You yourself have prooved what a harsh dictator is honor. No, Medford will meet Winthrop this very evening at midnight. And I would talk with you about that very serious event. Can you—will you keep Elizabeth away from the scene? It would not do for her to see her lover struck down . . . and, unfortunately, Charles has never been much of a shot with the pistols."

"Oh!" Halcyon's eyes widened in horror as the full implication of Dray's words reached her. "Poor,

poor Elizabeth! I will indeed do my best to keep her away, Dray, though I know not if she will heed my counsel. She is so very headstrong."

"Are we not all headstrong when in love?" smiled Dray wryly. "All except for you, Halcyon, who must have a heart of stone, I do declare."

"That is scarcely fair, my lord. I have to do my duty . . . Please do not make it hard for me! Can you not see that there is nothing I would rather do than copy Elizabeth's example and run away with you and live with you happily evermore? But would it turn out like that? Has Elizabeth gained happiness? Even if we successfully eloped, would we continue to feel happiness and no bitterness and remorse, especially when we looked back and saw the wreckage left in the wake of our own selfish desires? . . . No, Dray. It cannot be. Tomorrow I am determined to return to my father's house. I shall marry Rexdale's son . . . and you will find another . . ."

The words choked in her throat. She turned away and ran from the room. She thought she heard him cry, "Let me but explain," but she did not pause. She dared not listen to his pleas, dared not even remain in the room with him. She knew she would never see him again . . .

CHAPTER EIGHTEEN

When Halcyon entered Elizabeth's room that evening, the latter was sitting at the window, staring out at the falling rain. Her shoulders were hunched in despair, her whole posture evidenced her total dejection and desolation.

"Elizabeth!" Halcyon sped across the room and folded her friend in her arms. Elizabeth had turned at the sound of her voice, and a wan smile flickered across her lips, but to Halcyon's dismay her eyes were lackluster in her small, pinched face.

What a difference from the charming, lively countenance she had presented when Halcyon had first known her in her father's house in Grosvenor Square!

"Elizabeth, dear, what are you doing sitting here by yourself? You should not be in isolation at a time like this—you need your family and friends around you."

"Are you not forgetting, dear friend, that I have already cast off my family? I made that choice when I eloped with Winthrop. Shall I now creep back to them, having thrown the dirt of dishonor in their faces, and beg for forgiveness?"

"My dear, it cannot be as bad as that, can it?"

Elizabeth nodded. "Worse. Papa says he cannot bear to look at me, and Mama keeps on bursting into tears . . . It is better that I closet myself away from them."

"Then I am sorry for the smallness of their spirits, that they cannot forgive!" exploded Halcyon. "But I am still your friend, Elizabeth, for what it is worth. I shall not fail you, or forsake you. In honor or disgrace, the light of my eyes as they fall upon you is still full of love."

They embraced and shed a few tears.

"Do you really mean that?" Elizabeth said. "You are still my friend? You would do anything for me?"

"Anything," repeated Halcyon firmly.

"Then . . . come with me tonight!"

"Come with you? Where?"

"To the duel. It takes place tonight, and I have been ordered to remain here in my room. But I shall not! They cannot stop me now. Have I not already proved myself unworthy of their trust? They will hardly be surprised if I escape again," she said bitterly.

"I think it unwise of you to go," said Halcyon, remembering her promise to keep Elizabeth from the scene. "It would certainly upset Lord Charles to know that you were there. And if anything . . . goes wrong, why, it will be all the worse for you to witness it. Pray, consider again, dear friend. Were it not better for you to remain at home?"

"No! No! I tell you I must go!"

"But why?"

"Because I must!" She turned away and returned to her vigil at the window. "See, even Nature herself weeps for me tonight . . . Never mind, Halcyon, I—"

"Pray do not assume that I shall desert you," interrupted Halcyon. "If you do indeed intend to be present at this terrible act, then, of course, I shall be with you. I would not see you go alone. But, I feel bound to exhort you—*do not go!*"

"I have to! I have to! I—I love Charles, Halcyon. He is my whole world, my whole life. Without him there can be no existence for me. If anything happens to him tonight . . . I want . . . to be there." Her voice sank to a whisper. "If he dies tonight . . . then I die."

"Elizabeth! I hope you do not mean what I fear you mean!"

Her friend nodded. "If he dies, I die." She produced a pistol from her reticule. "I am prepared for that eventuality, you see. How fortunate that Papa taught me how to use one of these. I wonder if he will think of that when—"

"Don't! Do not speak so! I must warn you, Elizabeth, that though I will accompany you tonight, I shall stop any foolishness on your part."

The smile that Elizabeth gave her showed that she doubted Halcyon's capability to do that. No doubt she would have other tricks up her sleeve. Suddenly Halcyon realized that Elizabeth's grief and shock were likely to unhinge her mind; if ever she had needed a friend, then she had need of one now, and Halcyon determined that she would not let Elizabeth out of her sight until this ghastly affair was over.

Once again involved in intrigue with Elizabeth, she left Sir Henry's house as though she were returning home. Rebecca, awaited her in the carriage.

"Is Miss Elizabeth all right?"

"I am worried about her. She states that she has no will to live if anything should happen to the earl. Rebecca, she insists that I accompany her to this duel this night—I dare not let her venture there alone."

"Lawks, miss, that is foolish!"

"I know, but it cannot be helped. Now, listen carefully . . ."

Halcyon outlined her plans for the evening. They were to pick up Elizabeth in five minutes; she would steal from her room unobtrusively and would meet them at the corner of the street. Then they would make haste for the Crescent and Rebecca would go inside and explain what was happening to Lady Hensham. "She will be so worried," explained Halcyon, "And I am sure that we can trust her discretion." The carriage would convey Halcyon and Elizabeth to the appointed place for the duel between Lord Medford and the Earl of Winthrop. "I hope that I shall be able to persuade her not to betray our presence there, for I fancy that the earl might not take too kindly to her being there."

The preliminary stages went without a hitch. Elizabeth was picked up, having left the house without anyone seeing her or being aware of her escape, they dropped off Rebecca, urging her to follow them later, and then the carriage rumbled over the cobbles in the direction of the lower town.

The streets were almost deserted; only a few straggling merrymakers were wending their way home, a scattering of sedan chairs scuttling through the shadows, a stray dog, a lonely beggar on a corner.

They went down Milsom Street, skirted the Abbey, and entered Southgate. They were outside the city walls, and the huddling forms of beggars could be seen crouched near buildings or sleeping in the long grass.

Along Holloway they raced and Elizabeth stared anxiously out of the coach.

"I do hope we shall be in time," she murmured fretfully. "Hurry, coachman, hurry!"

The countryside opened out in front of them, and out of the carriage windows they could see the rolling hills darkly outlined against a rain-laden sky.

Elizabeth pulled her cloak around her and shivered. "It is indeed a dismal night for ghastly deeds."

They came to Beechen Cliff, and the coach slackened its pace; they swayed and bounced as the horses picked their way over the rough terrain. Then they stopped.

The coachman came down to them. "This is loik as far as ye'll go. Ain't no way uv going' further with them 'orses, miss! Shall us wait fer yer 'ere?"

"Yes, please. Do not leave without us." Halcyon shuddered. The murky, gloomy half-light seemed somehow inimical as though a thousand dangers lurked around them.

She gave Elizabeth her hand and pulled her up the hill to where flickering lights and murmuring voices proclaimed the presence of others.

"Remember, Elizabeth, we shall not show ourselves."

There were several reasons why she did not wish Lord Dray to see her. She had promised him that she would do her best to persuade Elizabeth to stay away from the duel, but she had warned him that her friend might not listen to her pleas. Lord Dray could not, surely, blame Halcyon for their presence here tonight.

They stayed in the shelter of the trees. They could dimly make out the figures of Lord Medford and the Earl of Winthrop, each accompanied by his second. Dray was there with Winthrop, their heads close together, and Dray appeared to be urgently speaking to him.

It was like a nightmare, a hideous scene playing before their horrified eyes. The antagonists met; Lord Medford's portly figure facing Winthrop's slender form. They faced each other, turned and paced the required number of steps, and then turned again and waited for the signal.

Halcyon felt Elizabeth's shudder. She put her arm around her shoulders, offering what physical comfort she could.

It was horrible, fearful! They waited with baited breath, not wanting to see the frightful outcome, and yet unable to drag their eyes from the two men. The swish of the soft-falling rain muffled the sounds. The signal rang out; two shots were fired. When the smoke cleared, it could be seen that both men were down.

With a shriek of horror, Elizabeth rushed from her hiding place and threw herself upon the prostrate figure of Winthrop. "Charles, my love, my dear! Speak to me! Speak to me!"

Elizabeth was convinced that Charles was dead. She cradled his head in her arms, pressing him to her as though she would never let him go. She was oblivious of all else around her.

"Lawks, my love," said Charles's muffled voice, "whose side are you on? Do you want to bring about my demise by suffocation?"

With a joyous cry, Elizabeth released him, gently running her fingers over his face, ascertaining that he was indeed not hurt.

"You are all right?"

"Grazed my leg; nothing more . . . Er—and Medford?"

Dray came up. "He took it in the chest. I fear he's done for," he said. "A sorry night's work, Charles, but it could have been worse—it might have been you lying there stiff and cold. Good God, Charles, I declare that's the first shot you ever sent straight in your life!"

Winthrop grinned. "My aim is pretty good when the odds are high enough," he said, gazing fondly at Elizabeth.

"I thought I told you to keep her away." Dray turned to Halcyon, his eyes cold and hard as flints.

Her heart sank. Of course, he was going to blame her for this, too. She let her glance fall from his. She could not bear those cold, accusing eyes.

"Glad you did bring her, Halcyon," smiled Winthrop. "It will save me the bother of fetching her. Got no time to waste now, you realize . . . I think, Elizabeth, a sojourn in France would fall very well at this time."

It would not be wise to stay. Dueling was not kindly regarded in these enlightened times. Dray assisted the hobbling Winthrop to a carriage. Elizabeth fondly kissed Halcyon and followed Charles with all speed; Dray helped her into the carriage, and then came back to that lone figure standing desolately in the rain. He came right up to her and then his eyes searched her face. It was as though he was impressing on his mind her image to last him for all time.

There was nothing angry or accusing in his gaze now. His eyes were alight with a blaze that laid bare his very soul; all the love, all the longing he felt for her were revealed to her gaze. She bit back a sob as,

247

wordlessly, he took one last look and then turned and went back to the carriage. She watched his tall, lithe figure walk away from her without a backward glance, and then he disappeared into the coach.

"Goodbye . . ." she whispered, but her voice was swallowed up by the softly crying night.

Halcyon sat in her favorite perch in the giant oak tree surveying her world. It had been a week since she had returned to Solchester. Her father had accepted her return with no awkward questions. She was glad to be back.

This is the real world, she told herself, not that phony world out there with all its false glamour, its pomp and wealth, its deceits and intrigues. This is the real world. I could live a lifetime of contentment here with the peace and harmony of nature all around me and never miss any of the things I found in Bath . . . Well, maybe only one!

She gazed out over the treetops, golden and orange and burnished olive now in the autumn of the year. She strained her eyes in the direction of the road; there was not a carriage in sight. Today she was expecting Rexdale's son to arrive. He had sent word to her father to expect him immediately.

I wonder what he will be like? Tall? Dark? Shall I like him? Will he like me? Maybe he will not come.

She sighed and began to climb down the tree, letting herself hang briefly on the lowest branch before agilely jumping the last six feet.

"You could get hurt doing that," said a voice nearby.

She turned, amazed, incredulous.

Lord Dray sat astride his horse in the very spot

where she had first met him. It was a hallucination! She rubbed her eyes and looked again. He was still there.

"W-what are you doing here?"

"What am I doing?" He alighted from his horse, threw the reins over a branch, and advanced towards her. "A strange question indeed! I thought I was expected."

"You . . . expected?"

"Yes. I have waited a long time." He held out his arms. "I have come to claim my bride."

"B-but . . ."

"I am Rexdale's son, my love, and I have come at last to claim you, to lay my heart at your feet and my life at your mercy. For without your love my life is worthless."

She didn't understand this great miracle, but she flew into his arms anyway. This was what she had longed for. The explanation could come later. His mouth came down to touch hers with a caress that deepened and flamed into desire. She clung to him as her one salvation in a loveless world.

"Do you forgive me, dear," he said later, "for the subterfuge and deceit?"

"Why did you do it?"

"Because, like you, I wanted a love to take root and bud without the cumbersome whip of duty lashing us from all sides. Then the longer I persisted in the deceit, the harder it was for me to tell you the truth. And Lady Hensham told me how you wanted just a small taste of freedom before you married. I was perfectly willing to go along with that . . . except that as I got to know you and love you, I wanted at all costs to save you, your purity and innocence and sweetness, for me alone."

"You seemed to hate me sometimes."

"A protection for myself and the way my feelings were taking over my common sense. When you told me there was someone else, I never even thought of myself. I thought immediately of Lord Charles."

"Lord Charles! You know now, of course, that I never loved him. I kept on hoping that, as your friend, he would confide in you and tell you of his love for Elizabeth. Then I knew that you could no longer suspect me of all those dreadful things. Did he tell you?"

"Yes, finally, but in such a way that I thought he was speaking of you. You see, he never mentioned Elizabeth's name. He told me—after Elizabeth's betrothal to Medford had been announced at the ball—that you had advised him to be honest with me. Ah! My dear! I thought immediately that, as I had always suspected, his secret love was your sweet self. I was consumed with jealousy."

"Why did you not tell me?"

"I did! Remember? You kept on denying it!" Dray smiled crookedly at her. "Was there ever such a mess?"

"No wonder you thought I lied to you. You had every reason to believe that your suspicions were true."

"Can you forgive me? Will you put aside your anger that I should have so deceived you?"

"There is nothing to forgive," she told him generously. "I know you had my happiness and well-being at heart. But how did you keep your secret for so long? Why was it that no one ever mentioned to me that you were Rexdale's son?"

"They were sworn to secrecy. All the world loves a romance, and all the world loves an intrigue, too. Combine the two, and anyone will help you. Lady Hensham ascertained that you merely knew of your proposed marriage to the son of the Marquis of Rexdale. She was sure that you had never heard the Marquis's son referred to as Lord Dray. So it seemed that we were on fairly safe ground."

A sudden thought occurred to Halcyon. "When you met me for the first time—here in this very spot—did you know who I was?"

"No. Not then. I was on my way to meet with your father, regretting heartily the fact that my days as a carefree bachelor were over. No more than you did I relish the thought of matrimony, especially to a girl I had never met. When I came upon you in the woods, your hair blazing in the light of the dying sun, your cheeks flushed pink with the excitement of seeing the fawn, my heart turned over. You were like a creature of the wilds, a wood-nymph dancing in and out of the shadows."

"And you kissed me."

"Yes." He grinned. "I did, didn't I? I confess I thought you were a kitchen maid from the manor. When I picked you up and carried you home—and you told me that Lucius Glaybourne was your father —Heavens! I realized I had met my future wife, and, far from dismaying me, the idea filled me with a strange excitement. You can guess the rest."

"And you came to woo me in Bath."

"In a roundabout way. Are you sure you forgive me?"

"I shall try very hard," she teased. "Although I think you should suffer just a little first. After all, you gave me a dreadful time, hounding me all over Bath —and then accusing me of selling my jewelry to finance my lover. I only wanted . . ."

"Yes, dearest, I know what you wanted the money for. You are quite right. I did hound you all over town. I did not dare let you out of my sight. By that time I was so hopelessly in love with you that I could not bear the thought of anyone else winning your affections."

"What a predicament, to be sure," teased Halcyon, blushing furiously as his ardent gaze locked with hers. "Let this be a lesson to you that the practice of deceit rarely does achieve the intended ends. Had you but told me who you were in the first place, I should have fallen into your arms, a willing slave."

"Say that again." He pulled her to him, and his hand gently lifted her chin so that she was forced to look at him. His loving gaze roved over her like a warm summer breeze. She could not doubt that he loved her as passionately as he claimed. His eager hands unloosed her hair from its restraining ribbons, and it cascaded on to her shoulders, whereupon he ran his fingers caressingly through the springing, silky tresses.

"My God, Halcyon," he groaned, "I would sooner die than lose you . . ."

His words reminded her of Elizabeth, and she pulled away from him slightly, as though determined to leave the full enjoyment of her own pleasure and happiness until after she had assured herself of the well being of her friends. "Did Elizabeth and Winthrop get away?" she asked.

"With all safety. By now they will be in France. And Winthrop has paid the debts Elizabeth's father owed to Medford's family. You can rest easy on that score."

He made as if to pull her back into his embrace, but still she resisted.

"And Sammy? . . . And his mother, and—"

"Be assured that they all all well cared for, too. Henceforth they will be in my care—so that there will be no need for you to pawn more jewelry, my love."

"Will that not be a great strain on your finances, my lord?"

"I think my pocket can stand it," he replied in amusement, reflecting how little drain they would be on his immense fortune. "But, enough! No more ploys to deter me from my purpose. I have a mind to kiss my future wife."

And, brushing aside all her halfhearted maidenly protest, he imprisoned her in his arms.

"We have wasted quite enough time already. I have been very patient, but every man has his limit, and I have reached mine."

His kiss whirled her out of this world to a place where only she and her lover existed, and his lips on hers were the only searing reality.

Then he swung her up in front of him on his horse and together they set off for their future.

Love—the way you want it!

Candlelight Romances

The passionate sequel to
the scorching novel of
fierce pride and forbidden love

THE PROUD HUNTER

by Marianne Harvey

Author of *The Dark Horseman* and *The Wild One*

Trefyn Connor—he demanded all that was his—and more—with the arrogance of a man who fought to win . . . with the passion of a man who meant to possess his enemy's daughter and make her pay the price!

Juliet Trevarvas—the beautiful daughter of The Dark Horseman. She would make Trefyn come to her. She would taunt him, shock him, claim him body and soul before she would surrender to THE PROUD HUNTER.

A Dell Book $3.25   (17098-2)